BAG

OF MINCE

There is no normal.
You just need to find your tribe.

Christine Hawkes

DEDICATION

To William, for listening to every word and not being like Alan.

CONTENTS

Chapter 1

Having the grandkids for half term was not something that Alan looked forward to. Everyone assumed that he had nothing better to do with his time, and that it 'did him good' to be out and about more. He had yet to see how; sitting as he was, in silence, in a cafe, on a damp Thursday in October, watching Nathan slurp his way soulfully through a carton of orange juice. To be fair, the boy was not really any trouble, it was just neither of them were great conversationalists and time hung heavily.

Alan drank the last of his coffee, put the cup down squarely in the saucer, stood up and began to put his coat on. Nathan read the signs and finished his carton with a final gurgle, exhaling noisily when he had drained the last drop. He shrugged himself into his anorak and looked up briefly to check for further instructions. Alan did not do a huge amount of eye contact, which Nathan accepted, but neither of them wanted to upset the other, so Nathan always tried to see what was expected of him. He judged from Alan's progress towards the door that they were off. Probably they would go to one or two shops, then back to Grandad's house.

There was no animosity between the boy and Alan, but there wasn't really much of anything else either. Having said that, today was not a good day for Alan.

*

He had woken up that morning with a feeling of dread that he couldn't quite explain, until he had looked at the calendar in the kitchen. 2.45 Dentist. That was it. Alan was involved in an ongoing complicated dental procedure which his dentist had assured him was vital. Three visits and £490 later, Alan wasn't sure they had the same definition of 'vital.'

As well as the pain and expense that Alan was expecting, he

would have to share the day with Nathan. His daughter Claire would be dropping the boy off just before 8.30, and the idea of the day stretched before him like a wasteland.

He padded over to the kettle, checking to see if there was enough water first, clicked it on and then while he waited for it to boil, he prepared the teapot and his favourite mug. He only had four to choose from, quite enough for his needs. Claire's older son Matt was off staying with his friend Callum, so at least he didn't have to worry about him today, but when they were all together, the four mugs all came out. Claire had the robin, what with her Christmas birthday, Nathan had the Land Rover, Matt had the golfer and Alan had the squirrel.

He didn't really like squirrels, but Jackie had bought it for him when they went to the Lake District, before she got ill and she could still do things. She liked squirrels, he remembered now, often noticing them in the park and pointing out their little hands and flicky tails. In the Lake District, they'd even gone to a special woodland reserve, said to have red squirrels, and they'd sat in a damp hide set up in front of a feeding station laden with squirrel-type delicacies. Twenty five minutes they'd sat, mostly in silence, but sometimes naming a bird or two that came to take advantage. They didn't see a single squirrel though, red or otherwise. Alan had wanted to try and get their money back - £4.75 each for nothing! - but Jackie said that he wasn't to be so mean and anyway they'd had a nice peaceful sit and spotted some nice birds and she'd seen a sign for a teashop just down the way. With poor grace, Alan had allowed himself to be cheered up in the teashop with a proper cream tea and had not even commented on the prices - £8.25 each!

Looking back, he realised that he had spent a large part of that holiday moaning and not wanting to spend money. Mind you, the weather had been miserable and he had been suffering with a sore ankle at the time. Admittedly, the sore ankle was self-inflicted, as he had twisted it whilst trying to retrieve some biscuits from the top shelf in his shed. That had been selfish, he thought now, especially as Jackie also liked that particular variety of chocolate chip cookie.

But then, she could always have bought her own.

*

So, here he was, just about to exit the cafe, and still more than four hours until the dentist. Alan paused in the doorway, thinking which would be the best route to take home. If they went left, they could buy the mince at the supermarket at a reasonable price, but if they went right to the butcher's on the High Street, they could look in at the model shop on the way. In a moment of uncharacteristic recklessness, and remembering his recent pondering on meanness in the Lake District, Alan stepped purposefully to the right.

As they walked, Alan caught sight of their reflection in the chemist's window. In between the special offer, diabetes screening, two-for-one posters, he was struck by what he saw. His own profile he was used to - its rather defeated sag and gloomy navy anorak was not pleasing, but at least familiar. It was Nathan's reflection that caught him off guard. He was suddenly so very like Robert. He had never seen it before, but just in that moment there was something about the stoop of the head, or perhaps the swing of his feet that stilled his breath. He hadn't had a jolt like that in he couldn't remember how long. He used to get them all the time - mannerisms of Claire's, a phrase overheard in the supermarket, even once the back of a boy's head on the bus.

He stopped to catch himself and regain his balance, mentally and physically, causing Nathan to turn and look at his grandad to see what the problem was.

"Alright, Grandad?" Nathan enquired, peering up at him and looking for clues on his face. Nathan was one of life's watchers, and often people thought he was a bit slow. He wasn't though, he was just taking it all in, thinking it through and filing it all for some later time. Nathan liked spending time with his grandad, although you wouldn't necessarily know that from looking at him. He liked the lack of demands that Alan's low-key approach placed upon him. Some adults in his life were always asking him what he thought and trying to engage him, but not Alan. Nathan knew that his grandad would not have chosen to spend today with him, and the feeling was

3

mutual. However, now that they *were* together, thrown together by other, more powerful forces (Claire) they were both reasonably content.

*

Claire often asked Alan if he thought there was something 'wrong' with Nathan, but he was doing alright at school and parents' evening always passed uneventfully. Not like Matt's! Quite a contrast there. Of course, academically, he was streets ahead of Nathan, but his behaviour was certainly more of an issue. He wasn't rude or aggressive or anything, just constantly larger than life and pinging off the walls. Perhaps that explained Nathan.

"Grandad?" Nathan tried again, having had no response. He wasn't exactly worried now, but he registered this stopping as unusual.

"Yes. Sorry. Just remembered something. It's fine. Right, let's get to that butcher's shall we? Pop into the model shop on the way?"

Normality returned, at least for Nathan, but something had begun deep inside Alan.

Chapter 2

The model shop, obviously the only one in the town, was at the top of the street that led down to the High Street. Many people looked at it from the bus window as they passed in to town, but it was very much a 'destination stop.' There seemed to be no reason for its placement at the top of a fairly steep hill, sandwiched between a bath showroom and a children's shoe shop.

Occasionally, children would beg their parents to take them in there as a treat for sitting and waiting nicely for new shoes, lured in by the shiny red planes and sturdy looking miniature tanks in the window.

However, once inside, they soon discovered that this was no place for a child. There was little room to move about in the shop, every spare inch having been filled with boxes of every type of model kit. The proprietor, Martin Rundle, kept watch of all customer movements from behind his custom-built shop counter. He had specifically chosen a local man, Phil, whose craftsmanship he rated highly, to build the countertop of his dreams, and he had done a good job. Using reclaimed timber from an old fire-damaged pew, he had fashioned something lasting and magnificent, fitted at the optimum height for Martin's somewhat diminutive frame. Following Martin's instructions, Phil had also made a cunning plinth, which added a full six inches to Martin's slightly unimpressive natural height of five foot five. Not only did this give him a clearer view of the shop, but it also gave him greater confidence and authority when dealing with customers.

The downside, as it were, of this plinth, was the obvious surprise of customers who required Martin to assist them on the shop floor. He found he was usually able to rise above this reaction, although he often constructed elaborate explanations about where certain products might be found rather than step down from behind his counter and be exposed as a shorter man than expected.

Behind Martin loomed the numerous small drawers that contained the many teeny tiny bits and pieces deemed essential to the expert model maker. All manner of specialist items were available for purchase here, but to anyone not 'in the know' it was impossible to actually make a purchase without somehow feeling inadequate and a bit silly. Martin refused to stock any kits that used the word 'easy' in their straplines, believing that model making's true purpose was to challenge and engage. He did appreciate that you had to start somewhere though, and had recently begun to stock kits that contained fewer than 300 parts and included the glue and paint you would need to complete them.

The inclusion of glue and paint had been a difficult decision for him, as he fundamentally believed that a model maker was only as good as his glue, and as such, one ought to buy the best available, separately. However, it was a move he was forced in to by necessity. Much as he did not like to admit it, he could see that unless a newer, younger crowd of modellers could be drawn into his world, his customer base would slowly but surely decline. The ravages of age - poor eyesight, unsteadiness, death - all these things put people off making models.

Consequently, Alan and Nathan were the first and only customers of the morning. Martin looked up smartly as the electronic shop door beeped to notify him of customers. He had been leafing through a hinge catalogue, lost in thought, and was rather surprised to see not one but two people.

"Alan! Long time no see! And who's this young man?"

"Hello Martin, yes, this is my grandson, Nathan."

"Nathan! My goodness, you've grown! Now, the last time I saw you, you were just a tiddler."

Both men paused and turned awkwardly away from each other, remembering Nathan toddling about at Jackie's funeral. Nearly nine years ago now, that would have been. Martin had been very good to come, Alan had thought so at the time. His own wife, Sheila, had passed away the year before, of an aggressive form of cancer, leaving Martin altogether alone. Much to their sorrow, they had never had children, but Sheila's mother Joan was still very much alive, and she and Martin went out for lunch on the last Wednesday of every month, hence early closing. Martin wasn't sure if either of them actually enjoyed their meetings, but it was nice to sit down to a proper meal in a nice pub and have a half of ale. Also, he didn't believe that either of them would be able to find the words to extricate themselves from this arrangement, so he supposed that he was still bound to go, 'until death us do part.'

"Yes, yes, where do the years go, eh?" Alan paused in the briefest acknowledgement of their shared sadness. "So, how's business?"

"Yes, well, yes, you know, ticking over." A blatant lie. Alan looked around the shop, taking in the vast amount of stock and air of stagnation.

"All looks great Martin. Remember that Spitfire you sold me, back in '87? That was a laugh wasn't it? Oh, the fun we had with that!"

Martin rolled his eyes, indicating that he did indeed remember that particular debacle. Fancy sending out kits with only right-hand wings! The company had refused to acknowledge there was a problem until Martin and Alan actually drove to the company HQ in Swindon with an affected model. That'd shown them! They'd had to eat humble pie then alright. Turned out they'd had some lad high on glue in the factory, couldn't tell left from right. It had never been clarified if the solvent use had been recreational or work related - they hadn't really thought about things like that back then. It even seemed ridiculous to think of the kits actually being made in Swindon, they all came from abroad now. Different times. Martin sighed deeply and focussed his attention on Nathan.

"So, young man, going to follow in Grandad's footsteps, eh?"

Nathan looked at him blankly. He was going to have to ask for clarification. Why couldn't people just say what they meant?

"How do you mean?" he breathed.

Martin's eyes flicked across to Alan's and then back to Nathan.

"Oh, you know, model maker? Engineer? Craftsman?"

"Oh. I don't know."

Martin's jollity faltered, then he rallied again.

"Well, maybe you and Grandad could try something together?"

Nathan looked beyond blank now, so much so that Alan felt he needed to step in.

"Yes, well, that's why we're here, Martin. Young Nathan's a fairly regular visitor at mine, what with Claire's work and all, so I thought we might embark on a little project. Is there something you might recommend?"

"Ah, marvellous. Yes, now, let's have a think. Now, I know you're a *plane* man Alan." Martin allowed himself a little smirk and sharp intake of breath, which Alan acknowledged with a knowing forward head tilt and a small eyebrow raise. It was an old joke between them, based on Alan being the opposite of a 'fancy man'. And also liking planes. Those were the days. "But what's *your* preference young man? Boats, tanks, railways, even? Eh?"

Nathan looked at the ground, hating this direct conversation, and the expectation that he could make such a decision at all, let alone quickly.

Time hung heavily while Alan and Martin waited for him to respond, and they exchanged tight but cheery smiles. Alan broke first.

"So, what d'you think Nathan? What shall we build?"

Nathan just wanted this whole thing to be over now, and was past caring if he guessed the wrong answer or not.

"Yeah, a plane, a plane sounds good. That one, yeah, great."

Both the men looked to where he was pointing, and their eyes lit up.

"Oh good choice young man. The dogfight doubles series has been most popular and of course, two planes in one box smacks of excellent value."

Nathan's face fell very slightly. He had no idea that he had picked something with not one, but two models to complete. If only he was more confident and didn't get so flustered when asked to make a decision.

His grandfather beamed proudly next to him.

"Yes indeed, Martin, a Supermarine Spitfire MK1a AND a Messerschmitt Bf109E-4-in the same box! What a knockout idea! Good lad, Nathan."

Nathan looked firmly at his trainers.

"So, what's the damage on that Martin?"

"List price is £21.99, but as it's you, I'll do it for £21," said Martin, looking over the top of his glasses, finger poised over the cash register.

"Bargain," ventured Nathan under his breath.

"Most certainly is Nathan, you won't get a better price than that, you know," agreed Martin.

"Right then, here we go," said Alan, ferreting for his wallet and locating the card he wished to pay with. He had a number of bank accounts, for reasons of security and economy, and it was important to him to use the correct account. This purchase would come out of his Nationwide account, chosen for its high interest at the time of opening. This rate had now dropped to 0.1%, but he had not yet got around to finding a better rate, and indeed did not expect to do so, given the current economic climate.

Martin dropped the box into a brown paper bag with a satisfying plop, and handed it to Nathan.

"Could be the start of something big you know. Good luck," smiled Martin, genuinely glad to have made such a satisfying sale. He watched Nathan as he left the shop, the door beeping efficiently in sharp contrast to his shuffled exit. *Just like Robert*, he thought.

Chapter 3

Seeing Alan with Nathan had affected Martin much more than he initially thought, and by the time he got home he had begun to brood. What would Sheila have made of Nathan, he wondered?

*

Martin and Sheila had married young. His parents had been keen on the match, as not only did Sheila seem like a nice girl, but her father was president at the golf club, and it felt good to be mixing with the toffs. Well, that's what Martin's father had said at the time, but Martin himself could not see any difference between his own father and hers, except that his own father did not own a blazer perhaps. He'd been twenty a few days before the wedding, but she was only just eighteen, so of course, lots of people assumed they'd 'had' to get married. Even his best man, Mike, had made several tasteless double entendres in his speech, some nonsense about shotguns and golf clubs, as he remembered it, but it wasn't the case at all. They'd been sweethearts at school, Martin waiting outside the Girls' Grammar to walk her home and just carried on from there. Sheila had left school after her O-levels, despite being quite bright enough to have stayed on, as her parents had wanted her to, but she'd had enough of school and walked straight into a job at Cooper's in town. She was taken on by Mr Cooper Senior as an office junior and did a secretarial course in the evenings. Mr Cooper Senior was a proper gentleman and always looked after all his staff, making sure that those who worked hard were noticed. The same could not be said about Mr Cooper Junior, a florid middle-aged lech, who seemed only to notice who was young, female and vulnerable.

On her first day, she had been warned about him by Betty, the partners' secretary.

"Never find yourself alone with him, love, he's got terrible wandering hands, and worse," she added darkly. Sheila, at sixteen, wasn't altogether sure what could be worse, but she heeded Betty's warning and kept clear. It was only some months later that Sheila learnt that she had been employed to replace Sandra, the last office junior, who had left under something of a cloud. Nobody would speak of what had actually happened but one day, whilst out taking the post, Sheila had been surprised by a rather raw-looking young woman with a pram, loitering by the staff entrance on Silver Street. The woman had looked furiously at Sheila, taken a poignant drag on her cigarette, then crushed it under her heel before steaming away down the street. She mentioned the incident, such as it was, to Betty, who told her the sorry tale of Sandra and Mr Cooper Junior. Seemingly, the two of them had been inappropriately close, and when Mrs Cooper Junior found out, all hell had broken loose.

*

Sheila was struck by the terrible unfairness of it all, and next time she saw Sandra, she made sure she caught her eye and smiled warmly at her.

*

After Sheila had been at Cooper's for two years, Martin felt secure enough in his own job at Benson's Engineering to ask her father's permission to marry her. He knew Sheila would say yes, but he found her father quite intimidating. Luckily, he caught him at a good moment, in the semi-private setting of the golf club bar one Thursday evening, where he jovially agreed to part with his only daughter and pay for a good do afterwards, knowing that the listening barman would be impressed with his bonhomie and good heartedness.

Sheila's father had been a Major in the war, serving in Burma, but it was not something he ever spoke of. Indeed, there was little he ever did speak of at home, maintaining an aloof and taciturn face behind his paper. However, at the golf club he was the life and soul of the party. Sheila never did decide which of these conflicting personalities best represented her father's true nature, and when he died of a heart attack three months after her wedding, she didn't know if she should be mourning or heaving a sigh of relief. Her mother, Joan, was initially appalled at being widowed at 40, but with the help of friends at the golf club (ladies having been allowed in since 1968, but only in the mixed lounge) she blossomed and truly enjoyed herself, organising events, putting together the flower rota for the arrangement in the foyer and of course getting rat-arsed on gin on a regular basis. It was not long before Joan remarried of course, this time to a much more like-minded man called Terry, who she met at President's Day the year after her first husband had died. They hit it off straight away, married and spent the next 30 years organising events, putting together rotas and getting rat-arsed on gin on a regular basis.

Sheila's death had been a huge blow to both her mother and Terry too, but they were of the generation that kept grief private, and so Martin always felt the need to pretend he was fine in their presence. Whilst they approved of this 'soldiering on' they also felt that he was not as upset as he might have been, which could not have been further from the truth. He had taken on the shop some years before, and he really threw himself into his work after Sheila's death.

Initially, he continued to see Alan socially, but after Jackie's death the following year the two men had found it hard to be together without dwelling on the absence of their wives and the friendship had dwindled.

He and Sheila would have loved children, but it just never happened. There had been a time when Sheila had cautiously suggested that they should look into adopting, but Martin had refused to engage in discussion and eventually she quietly let it drop.

*

As Martin let himself into his empty but immaculately tidy house, he felt Sheila's absence, as he did every time he put the key in the lock. Sometimes, he would be thinking of other things on his way in from the car, and he would experience a terrible dropping sensation in his stomach as he remembered all over again, that she wouldn't be there. Other times, he would think of things in the car that he would have liked to have told Sheila. Not anything big, just that Aldi's were doing garden stuff this weekend, or he'd seen the Evans' boy out on his bike again, or that the snowdrops were coming up.

Today, it was a lack of children that preoccupied him. Thinking back, why hadn't he wanted to consider adoption? He was not a particularly 'manly man', concerned only with producing 'a true heir', nor was he appalled at the idea of bringing up 'another man's child.' A lot of it had been about embarrassment and an unwillingness to discuss anything to do with sex. They had never had tests to see whose 'fault' it was, but he always supposed it had been his, as he knew he had had mumps as a little lad. He lacked confidence then, in fact still did, but he so wished he could have faced up to discussions they should have had. Losing Sheila had been... even now, there were not really words, but perhaps if they had shared the upbringing of a child who lived on, he could have borne it better? He allowed himself to imagine an alternative life, where they had taken on a child, perhaps two, and brought them up in this house. Right now he might be collecting his grandchildren from school, or popping round to his son's for tea. He looked bleakly round the kitchen to the window on to the garden at the back. Grey skies threatened rain and his deckchair had been uncharacteristically left out during the day. Better go and put that in, he thought, walking silently over the lino towards the back door.

Chapter 4

"Right then, butcher's, then home for lunch. Alright, Nathan?"

Nathan gave a nod, and zipped his anorak up more securely. He liked his coat a lot, and if fully zipped, it allowed him to feel almost invisible. It was very unlikely he would see anyone from school, but he couldn't take the chance that he might. He didn't class it as bullying, which he knew from anti-bullying week and other related days at school, was persistent and intentional. It was low-level ignoring, a clear reflection of the utter lack of interest his peers took in him, just the way he liked it. He didn't want to stand out in any way, or do anything that might attract the attention of the quick-witted cool kids who had the casual ability to make a joke at his expense. He found words hard and struggled to be able to gather his thoughts sufficiently quickly to engage in the banter of friendship groups. It had been alright when he was in primary school, as he had known everybody there all his life. They all knew him, accepted him for himself and automatically included him in whatever was going on. The hard bit had been going up to secondary school last year. It was a massive school of nearly two thousand students, but it had a good reputation and the bus went from just near his house. There were three other boys from his primary that went up at the same time, and he had been put in a class with one of them, but it hadn't been a strong enough friendship to be worth maintaining in the other boy's opinion. They weren't not friends, but also, they weren't friends either.

He also didn't want his name to be associated in any way with his older brother Matt. Matt, the live wire, risk taker, class clown. Matt, the mention of whose name made his teachers roll their eyes and smile. Well, most of them did, but either way, everybody knew Matt. They recognised his lanky walk down the corridors, noted his cheerful irreverence for uniform rules and marvelled at his exceptional speed on the running track. He was also effortlessly clever, or so it seemed to Nathan. How could anybody do so little work and still get top grades? It wasn't fair and it wasn't right.

Alan propelled Nathan into the butcher's shop, stretching his arm out fully to open the door for the boy. Nathan would rather have followed Alan in, but he had been given no choice but to lead the way. Not like grandad at all.

"Right then, Nathan, we need some mince. Here's five pounds, can you go up to the counter and ask for 500 grammes of mince please?"

Nathan stared at his grandfather in dumbfounded shock. Had the old bloke gone mental? Why on earth couldn't he do it himself? They were literally the only two customers in the shop, and any second now the butcher would come out from the back room, wiping his hands and grinning. What kind of moron would ask him to do this?

"Come on, you'll need this. Take it, Nathan." Nathan stared at the five pound note being waved at his chest.

"What?"

"I said, can you go up to the counter and ask for 500 grammes of mince? Please. Nathan. The butcher's here now. Ask him."

Words failed Nathan, as they so often did. True to stereotype, the butcher stood there, being jolly and rosy cheeked, but also a little confused.

"Alright Alan. How's you? What can I get you today?" he beamed.

Alan gave Nathan the tiniest of pushes and said, "Go on then, you ask now."

The jolly butcher looked uncertainly from the ever so slightly flustered Alan to the silent mortified boy.

"Nathan would like to ask you something. Wouldn't you Nathan?" persisted Alan, knowing in some way that what he was doing was wrong, but at the same time he was unable to stop himself.

Nathan picked his gaze up from the freshly mopped white tiled floor, looked his grandfather directly in the eye and hissed, "Buy your own fucking mince." He exhaled fully, turned where he stood and stalked out of the shop.

Alan and the butcher exchange glances. Their internal thought processes were both working at full pelt to try and make sense of the events of the past four minutes. However, they were both sensible men and knew exactly what to do in a situation like this.

"So, Alan, what can I do you for?" smiled the butcher.

"500 grammes of mince please, Stuart."

"Here you go, that's £4.75. Ready when you are," grinned Stuart, leaning forward with the card machine, Nathan having left with Alan's five pound note. Alan did not wish to break a ten pound note this early in the day and be saddled with a pocket full of shrapnel.

The machine beeped successfully, Alan took the proffered bag of mince (approximately a pound dearer than Sainsbury's, as suspected) and left the shop with a cheery "Thanks Stuart."

Curses, thought Alan, he would never be able to go into the butcher's shop again. He brightened almost immediately as he realised that the burden of supporting the town's small but struggling independent butcher's shop had now been lifted from him, personally. He would be free to buy his meat at whichever of the town's three supermarkets he chose without guilt or financial penalty.

As he came out onto the street again, Alan could see Nathan's back view disappearing round the corner, making his way home, no doubt. Let him go, thought Alan. Replacing his wallet, he brushed against Nathan's house keys. It was starting to rain. He turned his collar and set off purposefully after the boy. Seeing him at the end of the next street, he called out, "Nathan! Wait! Wait!"

This only made Nathan lean further into a determined walk and push his hands deeper into his coat pockets. Alan continued to trail behind him, but Nathan's speed walking was no match for Alan's older legs, bag of mince and brown paper bag of model plane kit.

A middle-aged lady slowed in a passing car to assess the situation. She looked worriedly from Alan to Nathan, plainly not reassured by Alan's friendly eye roll. She drove a little faster to cruise next to Nathan; she wound down the passenger window and leant across.

"Are you alright love, is that man bothering you?"

Nathan turned and shot a glance at Alan. He could so easily call "Paedo" now, and have Alan arrested quicker than you could say 'Jimmy Savile', but he knew that would be wrong. He briefly imagined the scene at the Police station, his mother weeping, school called, social workers engaged. He allowed himself a tiny huff of amusement, but said, very politely,

"Oh, thank you, no, I'm fine. It's my grandad." He smiled in what he hoped was a reassuring way, and waited for Alan to catch up.

"Nathan. You forgot your keys." Alan held them up to show the lady it was true. She looked to Nathan to see his reaction. He looked at her and said, "Thanks Grandad," then Alan and Nathan waited for her to go.

"Alright then," she said, not fully certain even now, "as long as you're okay love," fixing Nathan in her gaze.

"Yes thank you," said Nathan.

"Yes thank you," said Alan, simultaneously.

She checked her rearview mirror and drove away down the tree-lined street, leaving Alan and Nathan in an awkward no-man's land of possibility.

Alan broke first.

"Sorry. I need to explain." Another car, driven by a different middle-aged lady, slowed whilst she looked over at the two of them, trying to work out if she should be alarmed. "But let's get home first. Is that okay?"

Nathan assessed this person who looked just like his grandfather but was undoubtedly behaving in a totally un-grandad way.

"Okay."

They set off for Alan's house, wisely choosing to walk side-by-side this time. The middle-aged lady drove away, but they saw her looking at them repeatedly in her rearview mirror. Alan rolled his eyes.

Chapter 5

With each step taking them nearer to his house, Alan's mind was struggling with how he might be able to explain about what happened to Robert. It wasn't as if they didn't speak of him. It wasn't as if Nathan didn't already know that his mother had had a brother. That he, Nathan, had had an uncle who died in a car crash before he was even born. Alan knew this, Nathan knew this, and yet that didn't explain anything. His weird behaviour in the butcher's needed an explanation, and now was the time.

"Nathan, sit down. I need to explain."

Nathan kept his coat on, but sat down at the kitchen table. Alan sat down heavily opposite him, looking directly at the boy, who looked directly at the floor.

"I'm really sorry. About in the butcher's. I shouldn't have made you ask for the mince. I see that now. I'm really sorry."

There was short pause, then Nathan said, "S'Okay. Can I go now?"

Alan sighed, "Yes, of course, fine."

Nathan got up and went through to the sitting room without removing his coat. He put the TV on and shut the door.

"I'll be in here if you need me," added Alan lamely. His eyes flicked to the kitchen clock, and his heart sank even further as he realised that it was only an hour and a half till he had be at the dentist. He set about making some sandwiches for himself and Nathan - white bread, marg and cheese - and put them on two plates. He added an apple and a packet of crisps to each plate then called Nathan through for lunch.

"Take your coat off now, you'll not feel the difference when you go out otherwise," Alan said cheerfully.

"I'm good, thanks," shrugged Nathan pleasantly.

"Glass of squash?" enquired Alan.

"Yes please," replied Nathan.

On the surface, this was no different to any other day that Nathan spent with Alan, but they both knew differently. Alan tried again.

"Did your mum ever tell you about your Uncle Robert?" he ventured.

Nathan nodded, mouth full of sandwich.

"He was a great lad, very like you to look at."

"I know. I've seen his picture," Nathan gestured with his head towards the school photo of Robert on the wall of the stairs, taken a few years before the crash. His dark hair was swept across in a fairly low parting and he was smiling for the camera.

"He was nineteen when he died, but he hadn't been happy, like he is there, for a long while."

"Why?" asked Nathan, his interest piqued.

"I don't know. He just wasn't. He just gradually stopped being that boy in the picture, stopped smiling, stopped talking, stopped everything really. Your granny and I, we just, we couldn't, we didn't know what was wrong."

Nathan nodded. He got that.

"What did you do?" he asked, as he carefully put his sandwich back on the plate.

"We didn't do anything, we didn't know what to do. We just hoped he would grow out of it, I suppose, but then…; we did try and talk to him, but he wouldn't talk, wouldn't listen."

Alan looked up to see Nathan's clear gaze upon him.

"I think I was just worried that you were going to stop talking too, that you were too quiet and I was worried. I wanted to try and help you talk to people, to make you talk to people, but got it wrong. I just wanted to help."

"I'm okay Grandad. I'm okay. I'm sorry about what happened. To Robert. But I'm not Robert, I'm me. I'm okay." He directed a manufactured smile at his grandad. "See, I'm okay!" he said.

"Yes," said Alan, "you are."

"Right," said Alan, getting up and brushing crumbs off his trousers. Going to the dentist seemed like a pleasant release from all this. Funny how things turned out.

"Well," Alan continued, patting his pockets down to try and locate his wallet, "I'm off to the dentist now. Will you be alright here?"

"Yes," said Nathan, smile still fixed, "I'll be fine. Really."

Alan looked at him sideways. Nobody was fooled.

"Ok, well, you could always make a start on the planes, if you wanted…"

Alan nodded towards the brown bag on the work surface. Nathan followed his nod, checking that he had understood correctly that he was to do this in Alan's absence.

"It's all there, if you want to…." Alan tailed off and looked firmly at the floor. "Right, well, anyway, I'm off now. Should be back around four if it all goes to plan. I hope. I'll have my mobile with me if you need me."

"Bye Grandad," replied Nathan, busy with the last of his crisps.

Alan picked up his coat from the pegs in the hall, paused, thought better of it, and set off for the dentist.

*

Alan's absence was palpable, but Nathan went firmly back to completing his sandwich. Chewing determinedly on the malleable white bread, he wished again that his grandfather would do something about his television. Who on the planet still only had four channels available? How was it even possible to only get four channels, not even Channel 5? Alan must have done something to the set, or the wiring, or something, to make this happen. He loved his grandad, but really, four channels? Looking around, he focussed on the brown paper bag left square on the work surface, and rolled his eyes, again.

No wonder his grandad was keen on doing mental things like that with only four channels to watch. How would you even do that kit, let alone why? He pulled out his phone and idly googled 'Why would anybody even do an Airfix kit?'

There was no answer to this actual question, but instead, a number of videos offering advice and how tos appeared. How hard could it be? Internet time kicked in, and about forty minutes later, Nathan turned his eyes away from the screen to the reality of the box on the side.

Licking the remnants of the crisps from his fingers, he heaved himself up, took off his coat and set to.

Chapter 6

Meanwhile, at the dentist, things had not gone well. Luckily, Alan had allowed plenty of time for parking, which had been a nightmare. He had ended up in the multi-storey, which went against his principles, and then, having chosen the stairs rather than the evil-smelling lift, he had had to walk around not one, but two separate pools of urine on different floors. What was wrong with people? Actually, he already knew the answer to that. At the foot of the stairs, he had to negotiate the man begging at the ticket machine, and ended up giving him a £10 note as he didn't have anything smaller and felt guilty. He regretted now not using cash at the butcher's but although it felt something like payback, £10 still seemed a bit ostentatious.

When he arrived at the dentist, he checked in with the receptionist, who explained that they were running a bit late, but that the doctor would be with him shortly. This threw him, as he momentarily wondered if he had come to the wrong place in his rushed state, but then realised what she meant. It got him thinking actually - of course a dentist is not a doctor, but they must be qualified somehow-are they doctors of dentistry, or a doctor in the same way as somebody who is a doctor of philosophy is? He would have to ask Jackie when he got home, he thought, then felt that familiar stomach lurch when he had to pull himself back off autopilot and into the reality of her absence.

There was a TV in the waiting room, but it was set to Radio Inane, or some such channel, so there was nothing soothing to look at except piles of random magazines. He skimmed over the 'wimmins' ones and reached for the January 2010 issue of *Ships Monthly*. What a find that was! The whole issue was devoted to World Navies and promised to give information on the latest (albeit a little outdated now, almost ten years on) naval trends, fleet modernisations and new warships.

Alan was so engrossed in an article about the propulsion revolution in the shipping industry that he didn't notice that it was already 3 o'clock and he hadn't been called for his 2.45 appointment. The door to the surgery opened, and a blood-stained hunched figure was ushered out by the dental nurse.

"I'll do the paperwork for you Mrs Evans. You just get yourself home. Any problems, just give us a ring. Hayleigh, can you get the door for Mrs Evans?" she trilled, looking pointedly at the receptionist.

"Mind how you go now. Hello Mr Barnwell, be with you just now. Hayleigh, can you give us 5 minutes before you send Mr Barnwell in?"

Hayleigh nodded mutely, aware that something had gone on, but unsure of her role in it. She let Mrs Evans out and stood awkwardly to one side, as the dental nurse went clattering behind the desk and then reappeared with a mop and bucket. Hayleigh's eyes were like saucers now, she didn't even know they *had* a mop and bucket!

Alan had gone a funny colour, and it was all he could do not to run screaming from the practice as fast as his Hush Puppies would carry him. Hayleigh's training at the one-day seminar entitled 'The Perfect Dental Receptionist' finally kicked in.

"Alright Mr Barnwell? Won't be long now." (Recognise, reassure and what was the third one? Run? She knew that was wrong, but it was all she could think of. Reward? Could be.) "Would you like a sticker?'

Alan looked at her hard.

Maybe not reward, she thought. She gave a beaming smile and went back behind the desk. Alan stared into the middle distance of the Radio Inane screen and swallowed, whilst Foreigner continued to want to know what love was.

Just as he was debating what to do next, the dental nurse came back out of the surgery, clanking the bucket awkwardly.

"Could you just get rid of this for me please Hayleigh?" she sing-songed.

"Alrighty, Mr Barnwell, sorry for the delay. Doctor's ready for you now. In you come!"

Her body language and tone did not allow Alan to back away - she was a consummate professional and Hayleigh could only gawp and learn, bucket and mop dangling from her manicured hands. Alan didn't even have a chance to replace *Ships Monthly* on the coffee table, instead allowing it to be plucked from his nerveless grasp as the dental nurse ushered him forward to the waiting chair.

Approximately 45 minutes later in real time (and about 3 hours later in excruciating terror and pain time) Alan put one foot in front of the other and walked blindly out of the treatment room, through the waiting area and to the reception desk, where Hayleigh had recovered her composure and was busy re-alphabetising the dental products for sale. She'd struggled with there being so many 'ds' and was toying with the idea of moving dental floss to 'f' where it would stand out more and generally be easier to find.

Alan's slight topple to the left alerted her to his presence, and she spun round with a dazzling artificial smile (perk of the job) and asked him if he was alright there. He was, he said, he just wanted to settle up. This wasn't how it came out, but she got the gist of it.

She went to the computer and announced that it wouldn't be a moment, doctor was just putting it through now. She smiled again, but Alan was unable to return the courtesy. Hayleigh maintained eye contact but put her glossy lips together tightly into a twee smile and bobbed her chin forward. "Won't be a minute," she trilled again.

Alan looked awful, she thought, but all old blokes did. She raised her contoured eyebrows in a bright encouraging manner, then looked back to the computer where a ping had alerted her to the completed paperwork.

"There we are now, Mr Barnwell, just printing for yourself now," she chirped as the printer sprang into life.

Alan waited patiently as the printer buzzed out his invoice.

"That's it Mr Barnwell, just need your card if you will," as she handed him the bill. He felt sick anyway, so the size of the bill had no power to upset him further. He just wanted to get out, as fast as his trembling legs would carry him.

"Shall I get the door for you Mr Barnwell?"

Alan rolled his eyes and blundered out into the weak afternoon sun towards the multi-storey.

To be fair, he didn't think the treatment had been as bad as he had thought it would be. It all felt quite tender, but as the dentist (doctor?) had said, they were over the worst of it now. No food or hot drinks till later and plenty of painkillers and saltwater gargles. Take it easy, he'd said, and that was just what Alan had in mind. Until he remembered he had Nathan at home. He re-engineered his plan for recovery, factoring in the quick rustling up of a spag bol for Nathan. He inwardly flushed as he also remembered the purchase of the mince, but pushed that thought away and concentrated on getting out of the multi-storey in one piece.

*

Alan's jaw was starting to throb by the time he got back, but he put his 'cheerful' face on and prepared to greet Nathan.

"Nathan? You here?" he called, as he hung his coat up. "Nathan?" No noise at all, except the humming of the fridge.

"Nathan?" he called again, this time going on into the sitting room, where he immediately drew breath and stopped. Set upon Saturday's paper were two perfectly constructed models. A Supermarine Spitfire Mark 1a and a Messerschmitt Bf109E-4! Unbelievable. Alan moved in awe towards them, afraid to breathe lest he should break the spell. Their perfection! Their accuracy! The heady smell of fresh paint and fixative, combined with top-level pain relief, made him sway and stumble and he steadied himself on the chair back.

"Alright, Grandad?" enquired Nathan breathily, making him startle and turn to face the boy. Alan's mouth hung slackly open, and a little bit of dribble slid down the left side of his chin.

Tears welled up in his eyes and his skin turned an even paler shade of grey than before.

Nathan's eyes flicked over the situation before him. His grandad was clearly having a stroke (thank you PSHE Gods) or a heart attack. Or both. This is what old people did. All the time. Without further comment, he slid the chair around so Alan could sit down and pulled out his phone.

"It's okay, Grandad, I'm gonna call for an ambulance, it's going to be fine," he said as he started dialling.

Alan's face reorganised itself as well as it could, and he reached out to hold Nathan's arms.

"No, no, I'm fine! Been to the dentist! Just a bit numb, that's all. I'm alright."

Nathan hesitated, still waiting to be connected, and realised that he had perhaps been a bit hasty. "Oh my God, Grandad! I thought you were dying! Blimey, they've really done you over haven't they? You look really really bad."

Their eyes met, and the arm hold became a hug. A hug they held and savoured and used for their own purposes and each other's.

"I'm alright, really. But what about these models eh? I didn't think I'd been gone that long...." He tailed off, moving his gaze from the small planes to the (still small, really) boy at his side. Nathan was smiling! Really smiling! Looking down, and looking awkward, but his whole being was smiling.

"You clever lad! However did you do that then? I was going to show you how to get started tomorrow but...." he tailed off again in wonder.

"Oh, no, oh, I'm sorry, I didn't realise..." stammered Nathan, all the joy gone out of him like a burst balloon.

Alan was instantly mortified.

"No, oh, no, I just meant...it's amazing that you've done all this. It's fantastic. So clever! Come on now, tell me how you did it, I've never seen workmanship like it. You are one very talented lad. Exhibition quality, these are, and your first ones too! Amazing!"

This was quite literally the most amount of praise that anyone had ever heaped upon Nathan in one go, and it felt good. Weird, but good. He inflated himself again and allowed himself to bask in the adulation of his grandfather. He explained about YouTube, which took longer than anticipated, as there were whole concepts involved which Alan had to have explained to him, and about how it was easy when you could watch the videos, and how he had Googled any tricky bits. By the time the two enthusiasts had run out of steam, it was getting on for five.

"What are we having for tea Grandad? Mum's coming for me at six. Are we having spag bol?'

"Bugger the mince, Nathan, here's £10, run out and get yourself some fish and chips and a can of what you fancy. This is quite an occasion!"

"Oh, thanks Grandad. What about you? What do you want?"

"A sit down and a whisky I think. To celebrate your achievement," he replied, smiling at the boy.

"And your achievement too Grandad," Nathan shot back.

Alan looked at him quizzically.

"Not being dead?" Nathan answered.

"You cheeky beggar! Go on, get off to that chippy before I change my mind."

Chapter 7

Evening in Martin's house was somewhat quieter. He busied himself with small practical tasks and burrowed in the freezer to see what he might have for supper. The invention of the microwave was a godsend to Martin since Sheila's death, but she had done everything she could to prepare him for life without her. She had started to teach him to cook some basic recipes when she got her diagnosis, but she had only got as far as Shepherd's Pie and Beef Casserole before her cancer caught up with her and she did not have the strength to stand, let alone cook.

At first he had carried on with Shepherd's Pie and Beef Casserole as his staple foods, then he added in Ham Salad and then Quiche. However, at that point, he stumbled and resorted instead to the dizzying array of ready meals he discovered at the supermarket. He still had over 30 individual portions of Shepherd's Pie in the freezer, clearly labelled and dated (Sheila had encouraged him to batch cook in bulk and then freeze for convenience) but he was glad of the variety offered by Aldi and co.

Having selected a Mariner's Pie - cooks from frozen in 8-10 minutes - he put the kettle on. Mariner's Pie. How was that different to Fisherman's Pie? Or Captain's Pie? Or Admiral's Pie? Actually, he knew that one - Admiral's Pie contains prawns and often salmon too. The higher up the seafaring ranks you went, the more expensive the ingredients. That got him thinking. Shepherd's Pie. Technically, Shepherd's Pie should be made with lamb mince, although Sheila had taught him to use beef mince, and still called it Shepherd's Pie, not the more correct Cottage Pie. Cottage Pie always sounded a bit twee and forced, he thought, although major supermarkets didn't seem to have a problem with it. Hadn't there been a thing with horsemeat at one point - Stable Lad's Pie perhaps?

Having checked the freezer for peas to accompany his meal, Martin came back to his kettle and made himself a cup of tea. Like Alan, he favoured a mug tree, and all his four mugs were identical, a cheerful pink and blue floral pattern chosen by Sheila from a selection at Matalan. Matalan's, he should say. He and Sheila had always smiled at the local habit of transforming the giant retailer to a friendly local shop owned by a Mr Matalan. Before the mug tree, they had had a haphazard selection of mugs, collected over the years and chosen for a variety of reasons.

One day, Sheila had just come home with the mug tree and accompanying matching mugs and swept the others into a cardboard box marked 'charity shop.' She had gone through the house like a whirlwind, decluttering, she called it. Martin could only approve, having never really liked the more whimsical items in Sheila's china collection. He certainly wouldn't miss the wizened old man crouched on a tree stump cradling a pipe. No satisfactory explanation was ever given for its purchase, but when pushed Sheila said that she just liked it.

The sitting room became, as Sheila said, "a haven of peace and tranquility," with twigs in jars, scented candles and new cushions. Martin approved of the new minimalist approach, and saw that she would be able to dust that much quicker. He wouldn't actually have used the word soulless, but without Sheila actually in the house to champion her vision of clean lines and serenity, he didn't find the décor uplifting. The palette of grey and silver chosen by Sheila for its chic modern overtones now just looked sad.

Martin sighed heavily and retrieved his meal from the microwave. He continued to eat at the kitchen table, just as he and Sheila had always done, but he now used her space at the table to open up his newspaper and read as he ate. As a regular *Daily Mail* reader he was used to outrage and despair at the state of the nation, and today's newspaper was no exception. He read through it diligently, taking it all in as he ate his Mariner's Pie. Donald Trump and Meghan Markle dominated and a lot of nonsense he couldn't follow about some reality TV 'celebrities' and a moderately interesting article about Lindsay Lohan's mother. Whoever she was. In answer to his earlier unspoken question, he now knew exactly what was the difference between Fisherman's Pie and Mariner's Pie was - about 75p, but worth possibly as little as 45p in real terms and fish-to-sauce ratio. He wouldn't be making that upgrade again.

Once he had finished his supper, he cleared away and began his usual routine for a Thursday evening. He gathered together his till receipts from the special blue cloth bag he used and settled down in front of his computer. He had been an early adopter of information technology, and still had a large quantity of enthusiasts' magazines from way back when, stored carefully in the garage. He never looked at them now, with their helpful articles on 'Best budget floppy disks' and 'BBC micro - secrets revealed!' but equally, there seemed no reason to get rid of them either. Sheila had once or twice suggested he might have a bit of a clear out, but really, he kept everything so nice and neat in the garage, she couldn't complain.

The screen jumped to life in front of him, (he was careful not to leave it on stand-by) and he typed in his eight character, two-digit password, to include one special character and one capital letter. He then checked it back in the small blue notebook he kept in a drawer underneath the computer and fastidiously pressed 'enter.'

He saw immediately that he had several emails in his inbox, so he decided to deal with those before managing his accounts. There was the usual rubbish from suppliers, offering this deal and that special offer, but one was most interesting. It was from his cousin in New Zealand, Gerry, and he opened it immediately. He was very fond of Gerry and he felt quite excited to read his news. He and Gerry corresponded fairly regularly, sometimes reminiscing about their shared childhood in Martin's hometown. He, Alan and Gerry had all passed the 11 plus and gone up to the Boys' Grammar School together but then when they were 14, Gerry's parents had decided to up sticks and move to New Zealand. The boys had continued to keep in touch by letter for a while but things rather fizzled out once Gerry married and had children. They had reconnected quite recently through the Internet and both were enjoying the renewed friendship. Gerry had retired last year, having sold his office photocopier franchise business for a decent profit.

Gerry's email was light and chatty, and really lifted Martin's spirits. It was odd, but until he read Gerry's email he hadn't actually realised how low he felt. Everything in his upbringing told him not to make a fuss, don't stand out, be fine, but sometimes things weren't fine. Gerry chatted on about his three children, one of them was going to be a father himself in a few months. Obviously Martin was pleased for his friend, pleased he had such a busy life and was soon to be grandfather, but it put his own life into sharp contrast. The shop was not doing well, despite his chipper front to Alan today. Sheila would have been gone for ten years next month, and really, what was it all for? He could cut his losses now, just sell up and call it a day, but then he really would have nothing to fill his days. He sighed heavily and went back to reading Gerry's email. Gerry ended his email, as he always did, by saying how welcome Martin would be if ever he decided to visit New Zealand. He told him again about the 'garden room' they had, and how much he would like to see him and sit down together and talk about the old days. Martin understood that with age, a shared past becomes so much more important; a friend who you don't have to explain everything to and who watched the same kids' TV as you and played the same games as you became a truly valuable person.

A whole new chapter of his life began right at that moment. Without further ado, he logged on to his online bank account, using the log in details stored in his little blue book and checked the amount in his savings account. Keeping the screen open, he went to a new search - New Zealand flights. In less time than it took to cook an Admiral's Pie, Martin's New Zealand trip began to take shape.

Gerry replied enthusiastically to his email (having always been an early riser, Martin remembered) and gave him some possible dates immediately.

Before it was dark, Martin had booked himself a five-week trip to New Zealand, including a hire car and travel insurance.

Somewhat stunned, he tidied the kitchen and took himself off to bed. The following morning, after a restless night, Martin was up early. He got through his usual tea and bran flakes breakfast, tidied round and then set off for the shop, pausing only to pick up his rainproof blouson jacket in case of later inclement weather. He put the jacket carefully into the boot of his immaculate Ford Fiesta and having done a quick visual check (tyres, windscreen chips, bird poo – a perennial problem living as he did in a leafy cul-de-sac), started the car and reversed neatly off his driveway.

Chapter 8

Martin's good feeling lasted until a little after 10.30. 10.35 to be precise. He had begun to plan his trip in more detail, scrolling through maps of the area around Gerry's house, and further afield, as he was keen to make the most of his inclusive hire car deal. His phone buzzed and he felt a mild tingle of annoyance to see an unknown number come up. He was quite used to dealing with these unsolicited calls, and in fact was pretty good at spotting them and managing them effectively. Any other morning, he would have figuratively pushed his sleeves up and answered the phone with enthusiasm. Today, however, he was just ready.

"Hello, The Model Shop."

"Oh, hello, yes, hello, is that, er, Martin?" came a female voice.

"May I ask who this is please?" asked Martin, in his best formal-efficient tone.

"Martin, is that you? It's Carol."

Carol? Carol? He didn't know anybody called Carol.

"Well, 'Carol', if that is indeed your name, I don't know you and I won't be taken in by your nonsense. Good day to you."

He pressed the call end button firmly and precisely then exhaled with satisfaction.

The phone rang again almost immediately. Same number. Well, they were persistent, he'd give them that.

The hello he gave could clearly be heard to contain the smile of one who knows he's going to win this one.

"Martin, it's me, it's Carol, Joan's neighbour?"

The question uplift at the end of the sentence, and the mention of Joan's name brought Martin the revelation that this was not a scam. It was Carol, his mother-in-law's neighbour.

"Oh, Carol, hello, yes, sorry about that. Everything okay?"

Carol had only ever phoned in times of trouble. Last time it had been when Joan had locked herself out of her house and left her phone inside and he'd had to go over there with the spare set of keys.

"Oh, Martin, it's Joan. She's had a fall. You'll have to come. I've called the ambulance but they've said it might be up to six hours, and I've got a click and collect to fetch at 12 o'clock."

Martin was thinking, and he didn't like to share his thoughts until he had them organised.

"Martin? Are you there?" queried Carol, who didn't quite trust mobile phones anyway, and also felt that 5 seconds was a long stretch of silence.

"Yes Carol. What is her current position?" Martin wanted to be fully informed before he committed to anything.

"She's on her back."

"Thank you." He looked at the ceiling, paused for a fraction of a second and continued. "And in which room please?"

"Oh, she's not in a room, she's outside the front door. She was coming back from the Post Office and got into an argument with Ernest."

Ernest. Of course. How could it not be.

"I see. I imagine from the six hour estimate that she is conscious and breathing?"

"Yes, oh yes, she's saying that her hip hurts and there's no way I can get her up. I've put the little gazebo up for her."

Martin put it all together in his head and stopped fighting what he knew he would have to do.

"Right. I see. I will be with you as soon as I have made arrangements at my end."

"That's good Martin, thank you. Just to be sure, you will be here by 11.30 won't you, because of my click and collect? There's roadworks in town, and I don't want to take any chances."

Martin began to make plans for his departure. He decided it

would be best to treat the shop closure as a normal Wednesday. Which it most certainly was not, it being Friday. His busiest day. Apart from Saturday.

Although it wasn't 12 o'clock and it wasn't Wednesday (half day closing since forever) he always did everything in a certain order and end of day closing differed from a short-term emergency closure. Although he could class this as a short-term emergency closure, he could not count on being back at the shop by 5pm, so Wednesday half day was the nearest alternative.

He was just returning from the back room where he had unplugged the kettle and checked the lock on the toilet window when he was alerted to a customer by the sharp beeping of the door sensor.

He looked to the door and was surprised to see the slightly soggy but familiar form of his friend Alan, beaming from ear to ear, despite the drizzle. Following closely in his wake was the boy Nathan.

"Morning, morning, nice weather for ducks!" Alan began, clearly about to launch into something.

Martin raised his right hand importantly.

"I'm going to have to stop you there Alan. I cannot delay any further. Joan, you remember Joan? Sheila's mother? She's had a fall and I am required immediately. Apparently, I have to be there by 11 o'clock, so I'm going to have to stop you, I'm afraid. The shop will be closing in approximately five minutes, and there are a number of steps I have to take before this can be carried out effectively. I require full concentration and therefore, Alan, I wondered if I might ask you to step outside whilst I carry out the necessary tasks required for closing to take place?"

This of course, had taken longer to explain than to carry out, and Martin was willing Alan and Nathan to leave with every fibre of his being, looking pointedly towards the door, and gesturing with his previously upheld hand.

"Ah, yes, I see, not a good time. Poor old Joan. Anything I can do to help?"

Martin fixed Alan squarely in his gaze.

"No," he said firmly, but hopefully politely, moving Alan and Nathan physically now.

"Right. Well then. Well, let's hope she's okay. Give her my regards."

"Yes. Goodbye." He shut the door firmly behind them, turning the sign to closed, leaving them slightly stunned but thankfully for Martin, outside the shop. He was able to lock the door, set the alarm and leave within his specified five minute window. Traffic allowing, he should make it to Joan's by 11 o'clock.

Chapter 9

Arriving at Meadow View Gardens with a good half hour to spare before Carol's departure, Martin was able to park relatively easily, as fewer of the residents now had cars. This was not a reflection of an improved public transport infrastructure or declining wealth; it was simply because the residents were generally reaching a certain age. Back in the day, Joan and her late husband Terry had an MG Montego saloon parked on the driveway and an MX5 lodged in the garage for better weather, thrills and fun trips to the seaside. The Montego had been Terry's real love though, and although Joan had teased him about the amount of time he spent polishing it, she had enjoyed seeing the pride on his face when he stepped back, chamois leather in hand and did that funny downward mouth thing he did, implying satisfaction and contentment. The Mazda on the other hand, had been Joan's thing. She loved the tinyness of it, the feeling of zip and acceleration she could get even on the ring road. She had sold the Montego after Terry died, to a man who lived three doors down. With hindsight, she should have just sold it on the open market, put an ad in *Autotrader* despite all the hassle. Not because of getting a better price, but because of seeing it on the street. Or worse, seeing it *not* on the street, but around town, and every time, her heart giving a little lurch of recognition that turned to a hollow clang of realisation that it wasn't Terry driving, nor would it ever be. The man had moved away recently and Joan had been glad. Nice man, but just take the car away.

As for the MX5, she had carried on driving it unsuitably fast (for her age, for the occasion, for the road and conditions) until she had rather unglamorously pranged it on a bollard at the golf club. She was only there to top up the water in the flowers in the lobby and was mentally already on to her next job when the thud and crunch of metal on metal and plastic cracking pulled her up. The garage said she must have been going at 'a fair lick' to have caused that much damage to the car, and indeed it was impressive that she had reached so much speed in so little time, but that was Joan for you. Thankfully, she hadn't had Ernest in the car with her, but by the time all the repairs had been done, she had lost confidence and hardly drove at all. A few months later she'd had some tests done after a couple of funny turns (blacking out, palpitations, that sort of thing) and even though she felt fine now, she hadn't got her licence back and realised that her driving days were over. It was about this time that she and Martin had made a firm date of their once a month Wednesday pub lunch, which punctuated both their lives with such regularity. They weren't due to have lunch until next week, yet here he was, walking efficiently up the sloping driveway.

Carol had set up a folding chair under the small gazebo, and on the miniature picnic table she had placed a thermos, a mug and her handbag. She attempted, and failed, to get to her feet, not because she was old and infirm herself, but because a determined black and tan dachshund was sitting firmly on her lap, and looked as if he had been there for some time.

"Oh, Martin, thank goodness you're here!" trilled Carol. "I wanted to get myself organised, but I couldn't move Ernest, you know what he's like."

Martin did indeed know what he was like.

"Hello Carol. Hello Joan, oh dear, how are you?" he said, bending slightly at the waist the better to address his prone mother-in-law, whose head was just visible under the enormous pile of blankets that Carol had covered her with.

"Not good Martin. I heard it crack when I hit the concrete, side on. Carol's been an angel, but she's got to go, haven't you Carol? Click and collect you said?"

Carol nodded her agreement whilst making a mumbly positive noise and another poor attempt to get up off the chair. Ernest fixed her soulfully with his deep brown eyes and curled in deeper.

"Ernest, get off now, Carol needs to go," explained Joan.

Ernest looked at Joan and implied that her mental capacity was poor, and really, he didn't need her input at this stage. He was warm and fine where he was, why should Carol's needs be any greater than his? He tucked his long nose back in again and huffed, just to be clear.

"I'm sorry Ernest, I really am going to have to go now. Off you go, there's a good dog," tried Carol bravely, tilting her lap as far forward as it would go. If she thought she could dislodge him with simple physics, she was sorely mistaken. Realising that if the angle was any greater, Ernest might plummet, if not to death, then to annoying injury, Martin saw that he was going to have to step in.

"It's alright Carol, I'll take him," said Martin manfully. "Come on chap, there we go, " he said, reaching forward to put his hands around the sleek long body attached to Carol's lap. He quickly realised he could not get a purchase on Ernest without compromising Carol's privacy and delving much further into her lap than he was prepared to go. He blushed at the thought of what he might just have touched (it was her hankie, but Martin could not have known that) and stepped away quickly without the dog.

"Oh Ernest, you are a pickle," said Carol, more kindly than she felt. "I'm just going to put you down I think," she began, but quickly followed that with "on the floor, I meant," when Ernest gave her another mind-penetrating look.

He wasn't a light or convenient dog to move, with being so long and yet so short, but with some difficulty, Carol was able to place him without accident on the concrete, where he sneezed ostentatiously, smacked his lips and walked rather stiffly to Joan.

Joan smiled at him and used her failing strength to lift up a corner of the four blankets covering her. Ernest wagged approvingly and in a well-practised move he was in, under and settled within seconds.

"I'm sorry to have to leave you like this, but I'm going to have to go. Thanks again Martin, help yourself to coffee. Hope the ambulance gets here soon Joan, bye Ernest."

*

By the time the ambulance arrived, Martin had been told the whole

39

sorry tale. There had been a misunderstanding about mince, freshly purchased from that nice Stuart in the High Street (short pause for edited highlights of Stuart's life story to be related) and put for temporary keeping only in Joan's handbag, which she had put down on the ground so that she could better check her pockets for the keys, which she couldn't find. Ernest had noted her distraction and immediately gone straight for the bag, where he already knew the good stuff was. After discarding, but noting for later, a used tissue and a cough sweet, his hound ESP located the mince and ripped open the flimsy bag with one smooth movement. He was stealthy and cunning, but even a thief as practised as Ernest cannot eat 450 grammes of mince in silence. Joan had spun round as soon as she realised, but in doing so she made an inadvertent trip wire out of Ernest's lead, and down she had gone. Ernest had flicked his eyes briefly to her during the fall, but he wasn't going to take any chances on losing the mince, and just necked it even quicker, taking huge bites and no breaths.

When she actually hit the ground, Ernest had skittered away briefly to avoid being crushed, but went straight back to the mince despite Joan's weak cries. He did not stop until every last morsel was accounted for, licking the bloodied white plastic bag clean whilst holding it down with his paws.

When he'd finally finished, he had begun to move away from Joan, as he now needed to go and pee against Carol's flowerpots, a homecoming ritual that was long established. Finding himself securely tethered by his lead, trapped as it was under Joan's now unconscious form, he had no choice but to bark repeatedly for assistance, which was what brought Carol to the scene. In Joan's telling of the story, Ernest had become the hero of the hour, calling for help in the manner of a truncated Lassie, and he was happy to accept that this version of the story made her happy, which despite his appallingly selfish nature, was something he liked.

*

The paramedics were extremely kind, and Martin was impressed that it had not in fact been the six hours originally quoted, but a very reasonable two hours and fifteen minutes. Perhaps somebody had changed their mind, or they'd had a cancellation? He wasn't sure how ambulance allocation could be altered but he was just glad they were here now. Ernest of course had been a pain in the neck and had to be forcibly removed from the front passenger seat of the ambulance, where one of the crew had foolishly left a partially eaten BLT sandwich in its wrapper, and then barked persistently when Martin attached his lead to Joan's drainpipe. Joan weakly told him to be quiet, but this never worked, even when she was at full force.

"Oh Martin, you'll have to put him in his crate," sighed Joan, "keys are in my bag, I think."

Martin didn't think they were, but he looked anyway, passing fastidiously over the mangled remains of the tissue, soggy cough sweet (damn dog) and tattered remains of the beautifully clean white plastic mince bag, and then stood up.

"No, not here Joan. In your coat pockets, perhaps?" he enquired.

The paramedics had put all Joan's outer garments on the little picnic table, and once again, Martin found that Ernest had got there before him. Moist remains of tiny crumbs of dog treat were all that he could find in her tattered pockets.

"Not to worry, Joan, I have the spare set, I'll just use those." Martin dangled the keys reassuringly and, untying Ernest, took him inside.

He had never owned a dog himself, but he was familiar enough with Ernest to know that there were things you could do to manipulate him. He knew that it would be ridiculous to simply ask Ernest to get in his crate, and he knew that physical assistance would go down poorly. Going straight to the fridge, Ernest tacking along beside him, ever hopeful, Martin located the cheese, already cubed in a plastic lidded tub. With dachshunds on it. Of course.

Ernest knew the drill, and did what passed for sitting, a semi hover which kept his dignity off the cold kitchen floor.

"Cheese. Mmm," said Martin encouragingly. He held the cheese aloft, being sure he had Ernest's full attention. He walked on through to the back kitchen, more of a utility room really, but always known as the back kitchen, where Ernest's crate lived. Ernest trotted enthusiastically at his heels. Martin bent down and detached Ernest's lead. Ernest remained fixed on the cheese. Martin checked to see that he still had Ernest in thrall, aimed the cheese to the back of the crate and flicked it dextrously into the rear of the dog bed inside. It didn't really have time to land, as Ernest was in, after it and eaten it within less than a second.

Martin allowed himself a small triumphant smile as he closed the crate door. His satisfaction was only slightly marred by the volley of surprisingly deep barks that followed the closure. Martin knew that this was normal for Ernest, made some pleasant soothing remarks and went back to see how the paramedics were getting on.

Chapter 10

J oan was in the ambulance by now, but there didn't seem to be huge urgency to the whole operation. Martin didn't know if this was reassuring or not, but he was glad he'd shut the shop up properly using his full end of day routine. He had already established that he wouldn't be expected to travel with her and was beginning to think that his work here might be done. He could leave a note for Carol, but she had his number anyway. He was just about to communicate this to Joan when one of the paramedics came over.

"Right, looks like we're getting nearer to setting off here. We're thinking they'll be keeping her in, so could you put together an overnight bag for her?"

Martin made absolutely no response.

"Mate?" queried the paramedic, "just a few things....?"

"Martin, Martin?" came a reedy voice from the ambulance.

Martin looked past the paramedic to Joan, who had clawed the oxygen mask off her face the better to get Martin's attention.

"Martin! They're saying they think I might have to stay in. Blessed hip's probably broken. Honestly, it's such a nuisance."

"Yes, so I hear," replied Martin.

"So, Martin, right?" persisted the paramedic.

Martin gave a small stunned nod.

"What would you like him to get for you Joan?"

"Oh, you know, wash bag, my pills - they're all in the bathroom cabinet - toothbrush, change of clothes, nightie? There's a clean nightie in the bottom drawer of the chest in the bedroom. It's pink, brand new, still got tags on."

Martin nodded again and turned to go. He felt sick, he felt pale, his mind raced with images of the last time he had done all this. Not here, but on his own driveway, for Sheila.

Taking a deep breath and focussing on the job in hand, he turned back to the house, knowing that for the first, but possibly not the last time, he would have to confront his mother in law's underwear.

Having put together what he hoped was a satisfactory selection of items, he returned to the ambulance.

"Thanks Martin, I think we're just about ready to go. Joan's fretting a bit, about the dog?"

This brought Martin's worry about old lady pants back into perspective. How could he possibly have overlooked Ernest? A dog less likely to allow himself to be ignored he could not imagine.

Joan, practical as ever, had a plan, but she needed to run over the details with Martin. She explained that Carol would have Ernest in the immediate short term, but that she had already spoken to somebody who would take care of everything if such a situation as this arose.

"The number is on the fridge. You'll see it. Picture of a dachshund, Judy something. Thank you, Martin, you are good."

She extended a chilly hand, the one not attached to machines, and Martin reached out for it.

"Thank you, Martin," she repeated, "for everything, for all you did for Sheila, for all you've done." Her fierce blue eyes, made gentle and blurred by tears and pain, fixed Martin as best she could from the stretcher.

Martin couldn't trust himself to speak, but squeezed her papery hand. He understood. She understood. He nodded, then backed away. He watched the doors closing, and the ambulance moving away, leaving him alone on the kerb, until he could stand the barking no longer and went back inside to see what could be done with Ernest.

*

By the time Carol returned with her click and collect, it was getting on for 3 o'clock. Martin had been watching out for her car from the sitting room window with Ernest on his lap. Ernest saw her before he did and leapt suddenly and painfully (for Martin) onto the floor.

Martin felt pleased to think that Ernest would be Carol's problem very shortly. He just could not see why anybody would do this to themselves - the demands, the noise, the hair! - as he brushed off his trousers and went to the door.

"Carol! Hello!" he called, but was drowned out by Ernest's frantic barking.

"Oh hello, little chap, shush now, there we are, it's okay," soothed Carol, as Ernest rushed into her car. He barged straight past her to the back seat where her fortnightly food shop was sitting. Almost immediately, he was in one of the bags, his tail whipping left and right, signalling success on the perpetual crusade for food that was Ernest's life.

"Ernest! No, no! Stop that! Right now!"

Nothing that Carol said made the slightest difference, so she hefted herself out of the driver's seat and flipped it forward the better to get him out.

In between admiring Carol's swift actions and her extracting the protesting Ernest, Martin silently congratulated himself on having a five-door car.

"You are a very naughty dog, young man," said Carol, allowing herself to be licked under her chin. "Oh, mind my earrings! Oh Ernest!" as Ernest did what he did best - go too far with everything.

She put him down on the driveway, being careful to shut her car door. He sneezed and went straight to pee on the plant pot by her front door.

"Did Joan get off alright? I'm sorry I had to leave you like that. It all took longer than I thought, it was my first go at click and collect, so I had to have a coffee afterwards, you know how it is."

Martin did not, but it confirmed to him what he had long suspected about click and collect.

*

Martin relayed what the ambulance crew had told him and Carol agreed that she had thought it was probably a broken hip too. Martin asked if she had a medical background and she explained that whilst she did not, she was a keen watcher of 'anything medical' on the telly. They chatted a little more, then, having exhausted the details of Joan's departure, their mutual gaze fell to Ernest, who was whining at his own door.

"So. Ernest. Joan said you would be able to have him tonight. She's got somebody lined up for longer term, Judy something?" He looked at her enquiringly to see if Carol knew Judy Something, but her expression said not, so he continued. "Her number's on the fridge but I haven't phoned her yet..."

Martin trailed off, sensing Carol backing away both physically and emotionally.

"Oh no, Martin. No, sorry, no. I can't think why she would have said I'd have him. It's not that he's not a lovely dog, but I've got my cat to think of. She's nearly 16 and I can't have her upset. She'll be peeing everywhere, scratching up the curtains and, no, sorry, but just no."

"Right. Yes. I see how that might be tricky."

They stood there, watching Ernest who had found a sunny spot on the concrete and was lying flat on his side, oblivious to the discussion above him.

Carol could see that Martin was struggling and she felt sorry for him.

"Let me put this shopping away, then I'll come over and we'll make a plan."

"Thank you, Carol. I'll put Ernest in his crate and help you with those bags."

Martin carried out the treat/crate manoeuvre and once the shopping was safely at Carol's, they sat down together with a cup of tea and Judy Something's number.

Chapter 11

The following morning, although a bright and sunny Saturday, did not bring a cheerful dawn to Martin's house. He had had what could only be described as a difficult night with Ernest, who he had been forced to bring home with him, following no response whatsoever from Judy Something, despite the leaving of three voice messages and one carefully worded text requesting her urgent attention.

He had erected the crate, stored the dog food securely, fed and walked Ernest successfully and settled him in the kitchen. All had gone far better than could be expected. Martin had begun to suspect that all Ernest needed was firm boundaries and clear rules, given out by a calm concise person such as himself. Joan was a very nice person, but really, she had let Ernest rule the roost.

Martin had switched off the lights and went upstairs. He had already decided that if Ernest did bark, he would ignore it. The dog would soon see that resistance was futile and all would be well.

By the following morning, Martin had advised Ernest to stop barking seven times, gone downstairs eight times and been disturbed constantly by the dog shifting position around, on and finally in the bed which Martin had eventually been forced to share with him.

To say that 6.30 was when Martin woke up would be inaccurate, as he felt as if he had never truly slept at all. 6.30 was when Martin moved into a greater awareness of his surroundings and opened his eyes. He sighed deeply and reached under the duvet to rest his hand on the sleek hot body of Ernest, lying flush to his tartan pyjama-ed leg, bony head upon bony calf. Martin pulled back the duvet and got up wearily, looking down at the prostrate dachshund. Ernest gave him an indulgent side eye and wagged his tail thumpily on the mattress. He showed no sign of moving. Martin pointed wordlessly to the door, his shoulders sagging with resignation. Ernest flipped over seductively and curled into a slinky C-shape. Martin scooped him up and carried him downstairs to begin their first full day together.

Martin had already decided that Ernest would stay home whilst he went to the shop. Saturday was his busiest day and he couldn't be doing with having a dog under his feet. He left one more voice message with Judy Something (he hoped to find out her second name at some point, soon) put Ernest in the crate and left the house in the usual way. Carol had told him that Ernest would be quite alright left for a few hours and he planned to pop back and let him out towards lunchtime, when he could reasonably put a 'Closed for lunch' sign up for 20 minutes.

He had been open for about 25 minutes when the door beeped out its warning, and in walked Alan and Nathan. They were still smiling.

"Morning Martin, okay to come in?" Alan ventured, as he looked expectantly at Martin.

"Of course, come in. We are very much open for business today. And before we go any further, I would like to apologise for hurrying you out of the shop yesterday. Not often I get called away like that, and you were most understanding."

"Oh no, that's fine. How is she anyway? All alright?"

"Yes, broken hip they think. I'm not sure if they need to operate at all, but I phoned the hospital this morning and they said they would know more later. They've got my mobile, the home number and the shop, so I expect them to reach me."

Alan nodded encouragingly, as if waiting for more news.

"So, yes, she's alright, thank you Alan."

An awkward pause was about to develop, but Alan stepped up to the plate.

"So, the planes we bought, Nathan and I, the other day..." Alan looked pointedly towards his grandson, coat zipped up, carrier bag in hand. Martin interpreted this second pause as Alan being about to make a complaint. He felt he knew the signs. He stood a little taller on his plinth, and let his reading glasses drop slightly down his nose...

Alan was waiting for Nathan to produce the completed models from his carrier bag. They had discussed in detail how they would carry out the big reveal and the exact signal that Alan would give for it to take place. Alan had wanted to wink, but Nathan felt that this was an outdated signal (lame, was what he actually said) and what if Alan got something in his eye at a different time and, well, it just wasn't clear enough. In the end, they had agreed on a clear verbal communication.

"Nathan, please get the planes out of the bag and put them there in front of Martin."

Nathan did exactly that, but it took a little while because of the bubble wrap and the bag handles.

Martin was suitably impressed.

"Oh, yes. Well done. These are excellent quality Alan, you haven't lost your touch, and so quickly too." He continued to examine the models, looking with his eyes and his hands the better to soak in their perfection. Remembering the boy at Alan's side, Martin said encouragingly, "And I bet you helped your grandad didn't you?"

Nathan wrestled free of his hood, wiped his fringe away and breathed.

"Actually, I did them both myself. On my own? When Grandad was out."

Alan could have popped with pride. Martin merely took off his reading glasses.

"Well, well, young man. I do beg your pardon. I take my hat off to you."

Nathan looked briefly at Martin's bare head, then took the compliment he thought he was probably being given.

"These really are good. The joints and paintwork are superb. Well done, young man, well done."

"Thank you, Mr Rundle," began Nathan, but he was interrupted.

"Martin, please. To a fellow model enthusiast. Call me Martin."

"Oh. Okay." Nathan hadn't factored this in, but carried on regardless.

"So, Martin. Please can you suggest what I should make next?" He and his grandad had discussed all of this, and so far, apart from the Mr Rundle/Martin thing, it was going pretty much to plan.

Martin's eyes lit up. What a question for a Saturday morning, especially after such a fraught Friday day and night. Where should he direct the boy? What would be best?

"Well, I think we can dispense with any further starter sets," chuckled Martin, "Does it have to have wings, or are you ready for anything?"

Alan was on hand to interpret this before Nathan could get flustered.

"No, no, Nathan is happy to be guided by you, whatever you might think."

"Mmm, now, I'm going to put out a few options on the counter and you can decide from there," proposed Martin, but Nathan stopped him.

"Thank you, erm, Martin, I don't really like choosing, so if you could pick for me, that would be good."

Martin looked surprised and checked for confirmation from Alan.

"Yes please, Martin, anything up to around the £40 mark."

Nathan put his hood back up and waited whilst Martin came out from behind the counter and bustled around the shop. He was quite surprised how tall Martin wasn't, and furtively leant back so he could see around the back of the counter and observe what it was that Martin had been standing on. Nice plinth.

Alan and Nathan exchanged straight-smiled eyebrow raises and waited. After some further minutes, Martin returned to his position behind the counter and placed a single box in front of Nathan.

"Ticks all the boxes, this does. Reputable manufacturer. Skill rating of 2-4, historically interesting and under £40. The end result will be a stunning 1:700 scale model of the world's best known 'unsinkable' ocean liner. Before she sank, obviously."

Nathan looked closely at the box.

"RMS Titanic. Cool."

Martin was just finalising the payment when the shop phone rang.

"Oh, just a moment, I expect that'll be the hospital. I'll just answer it if you wouldn't mind." Nathan and Alan nodded in agreement, and waited.

"The Model Shop, Martin Rundle speaking. How may I help you?"

A long silence, during which Martin's face went from expectant to concerned to saggy.

"Yes, I see."

More saggy silence.

"No, I quite understand."

Slightly braced sagging, and a tiny shoulder lift.

"Yes, I see. I'll be there shortly. Thank you."

He put the phone down and inhaled deeply.

"Oh, dear. Joan?" Alan asked kindly.

"No Alan, it's Ernest."

*

Martin explained the situation as best he could to Alan and Nathan. It took a while for it to make sense and for them to understand that Susie and John were Martin's near neighbours and who Ernest was and why he was Martin's responsibility, but eventually Alan had a rudimentary grasp of the problem.

"So, do you have to go home and fetch him now, or can it wait till after closing time?"

"John said that Susie's had a major flare up. Normally, bin day isn't a problem, but the dog barking has really pushed her over the edge. It's surprising how sound carries in a cul-de-sac."

Alan was shocked.

"Bin day? Surely not. It's Saturday!"

"Obviously bin day is not today Alan. John was referring to the stress caused by bin day *yesterday. Friday.* Recycling day is often much worse for Susie," he added enigmatically. He had never actually met Susie, known semi- affectionately on the close as 'Loony Susie', but she was often referenced among his neighbours and he once thought he had seen a shadow at the windows that might have been her, but in this instance he understood her pain. "And now the dog has been barking since I left and she just can't take it. I am required to go home and fetch Ernest. I have no alternative but to bring him here." Martin looked forlornly about the shop, imagining his temple to order and organisation being defiled by Ernest's presence.

The third pause of the day allowed everyone to take stock.

"I've got a delivery coming at 11 o'clock, and there are several customers I am expecting today, to say nothing of the passing trade."

They all looked out onto the empty street.

Martin continued, "I am afraid I am going to have to ask you to vacate the premises once again, as I will have to shut the shop and fetch Ernest."

Nathan tugged delicately on Alan's anorak sleeve.

"Grandad, couldn't we go and fetch Ernest?" Nathan loved dogs, but had never been allowed to have one, because of Claire's work.

Alan was stunned. Not only was Nathan speaking without prompting, but he was offering an active solution to a problem that was actually happening right now. He hadn't needed time to mull over this one.

"Absolutely. Yes, we could do that. What about that, Martin? Would that help?"

Martin saw that this was a genuine offer which would get him out of a tricky situation. Some key-related business was conducted between the men, and Martin promised to look after the planes and keep a hold of the *RMS Titanic*.

Nathan snuffled out a giggle, looked up and said, "Yeah, watch out for icebergs, Martin," which everybody found surprising and amusing in equal measure before they pinged their way out of the shop.

Chapter 12

The 20-minute walk to Martin's house passed uneventfully, on the surface. Nathan had stopped following Alan, and was now walking alongside him. It would be wrong to say that conversation flowed - it didn't - but there were small bursts of communication between the two. Communication centred initially on a shared interest in the proposed re-building of the Titanic. This led almost naturally, like a raindrop falling down a windowpane, to sharing of Titanic-based facts. The communication paused, grew and then - once enough information had been gathered and pooled - overflowed, trickling downwards, pulling in other droplets as it went. It wasn't effortless, it was comfortable, but they had both given in to gravity.

As they turned the corner into Martin's road, a tall hugely-built man leapt forward from the street sign he had been sitting on. He was clearly expecting Martin and tried to hide his disappointment by putting his hands into his pockets, but it was obvious, especially to Nathan, that they had let him down. Nathan knew this man. He knew what his body did in times of frustration, in times of burnt hope and in times of drilling boredom. This man was his chemistry teacher, Mr Peterson. Nathan put his hood up stealthily and slotted in behind Alan.

"Morning!" said Alan cheerily, "Just on our way to fetch the dog from number 23. I'm Martin's friend, Alan?"

The man removed his hands from his pockets, in what Nathan knew was a gesture of triumph and delight. He hadn't often seen it, but there had been that time when Kyle had been unexpectedly removed from the lesson by the deputy head, and another occasion when the fire alarm had gone off five minutes into a double lesson.

"Oh, yes, that is good. Yes, very good. Have you got a key?" He touched his collar gently, alerting Nathan to the fact that everything was riding on Alan's answer. It was a gesture familiar to all his students, and even seeing it now, outside of school, made Nathan's heart race a little faster and hope he might be able to use Martin's toilet.

"Indeed I have." Alan dangled the key encouragingly towards Mr Peterson, who actually smiled. This was a new one for Nathan.

The lull in conversation allowed all three of them to notice the dog barking, persistently, from number 23. Mr Peterson looked anxiously away towards number 25, his own house. The curtains were all drawn, despite the lateness of the hour and the sunniness of the morning. Nothing moved, but Alan and Nathan turned too, to see what he was looking at. Nothing to see for sure, but they all felt it, a tension, and an expectation that all was not well.

"Right well, mustn't keep you, Mr er..."

"Barnwell, Alan Barnwell."

John actually looked at Alan now. And at Nathan, briefly.

"Right, yes, sorry. John Peterson. Thanks for coming."

Alan gave a pleasant nod of acknowledgement and he and Nathan went to go and sort the dog out.

There was no obvious reason for Ernest's extended barkathon, except that he objected to being incarcerated and left alone. Released, he became the life and soul of the party, instantly attaching himself to Nathan, mentally and physically. The attachment was immediately mutual, and by the time Alan had found the lead, the poo bags and the treats that Martin said were essential for motivating Ernest, boy and dog were one.

By the time they came out of the house, the street was completely deserted, but neither Alan nor Nathan were aware of anything except the dog, who high stepped happily alongside Nathan, looking up and ahead eagerly to the next lamppost on the corner. Alan stepped back mentally, just enough to savour the connection between this boy - no, *person* - and this little creature. They were both so alive, so present and so full of enthusiasm. This was what he had wanted to see in the butchers, but seeing it now, for real, he marvelled at his own stupidity and smiled.

*

Martin was busy serving a customer when they got back to the shop, but was able to give them a brief acknowledgement in between explaining why the customer's choice of glue was not going to be suitable for the project he had in mind. The customer took it surprisingly well and the sale was concluded in a way that was satisfactory to all parties.

Ernest strained on the lead to explore the shop while Martin eyed him suspiciously from his plinth, at which point the phone rang.

"Excuse me," said Martin. "I shall have to answer that, as it could well be the hospital ringing about Joan. I'll answer it just now, if you don't mind. Excuse me, if you will."

Alan agreed that answering it would be quite acceptable to him, so Martin answered the phone.

"The Model Shop, Martin Rundle speaking. How may I help you?"

It was the hospital, and it was about Joan. Martin made some notes and seemed in turns, unsurprised, solicitous and resigned. Alan did not wish to appear to be listening but really had no choice in the matter. Martin pressed the call end button firmly and replaced the phone in its cradle carefully. He sighed and straightened his notepad. Alan returned plinth-wards and asked if everything was okay.

It was, and it was not. Joan was stable but would require an operation, due to happen as soon as a theatre became available. She was being given painkillers to manage the pain and they would keep Martin informed. She would be in for at least a fortnight and very possibly longer. Martin was a kind man and he certainly felt sorry for Joan, but he was also a practical man, and immediately his thoughts turned to the dog. And why Judy Something had still not called him back. He really needed to call her again. He also really needed some quiet reflective time to compose what he was going to say to her, if and when she answered her phone, but as Nathan was lying on the floor helping Ernest to investigate something that was lodged underneath a display of Humbrol enamel paints, he was somewhat distracted. Alan came to his rescue.

"Nathan? What about taking Ernest to the park for half an hour?"

Nathan reverse camo-crawled out from under the unit and pushed his hood back to better hear and see. Ernest was still otherwise engaged under the ominously rattling stand.

"Yeah, sure. I'll keep him on his lead. Come on Ernest," he said, simultaneously rustling the treat bag, which had an immediate effect. The display stand gave a final lurch then shuddered to a standstill as Ernest showed that he was ready to be otherwise entertained.

For the second time that day, Martin had to explain a cast of characters, their motives and actions so far. Alan thought he might already know Carol, but it turned out to be a different Carol, as the one he knew didn't drive and this one did, but once this was cleared up, they were able to move on and work together on the whole Judy Something issue. Alan did actually know somebody called Judy who was into dogs, but she had been a friend of Jackie's from school days and she lived in Devon now, he thought, so it might not be the same one, but then again, you never knew, small world and so on.

Both men waited expectantly for the call to go through and whilst Martin fully expected it to go to voicemail again, he was delighted but a little flustered when an actual person answered. There was a lot of background barking going on, so he was hopeful that he was on the right track, but it did make communication challenging. As soon as she got his name, she apologised profusely for not getting back to him sooner. She explained that things had been a bit fraught at her end and that she'd never known kennel cough spread so quickly. All eight of her own dachshunds (she pronounced it dash-uns) and two of the rescues so far had all gone down with it.

The long and short of it was, in between volleys of hoarse barking, that there was no way she could take Ernest for the foreseeable future. She was very apologetic and sent her best wishes to Joan, but couldn't offer any more than that.

This was obviously not what Martin had been hoping for. He had really thought that getting hold of Judy Something (still no clue as to her surname) would have been the end of his Ernest-related worries. He suspected that it was in fact, just the beginning.

Chapter 13

Taking a dog to the park, alone, featured high up on Nathan's list of things he'd like to do but had never actually formed into a specific thought. All traces of the self-conscious embarrassment he usually felt walking anywhere melted away. He focused fully on the sleek little dog at the end of the lead. He didn't notice his trainers, he forgot to put up his hood or even zip up his anorak. He made sure to respect Ernest's interests and let him sniff and stop for as long as he liked. Ernest quickly capitalised on this and the short walk to the park took twice as long as it should, but it really wasn't a problem.

The nearer they got to the park, the more animated Ernest became. He stretched the lead to full capacity, forcing the delighted Nathan into a happy trot. Running along together, through the park gates and along the tarmac paths, felt freer to Nathan than anything else he had ever experienced. Ernest, who contrived above everything else to do exactly what he wanted to, when he wanted to, felt rather constrained. He started to make whistling noises and puff air out of the sides of his mouth, straining ahead even though Nathan was running at full pelt. He led Nathan at speed to an overflowing bin, and it was only by extreme quick thinking (Nathan? Quick thinking?) that Nathan was able to stop him eating a discarded tuna sandwich that was wedged around the back of the adjacent bench.

Nathan realised that Ernest needed distraction, and with the aid of the treats bag, he was able to get him away from the sandwich and off into open ground. It was hard to be spontaneous and fun on such a short lead, but Ernest couldn't help but join Nathan on his romp through the fallen leaves and soon began to properly enjoy himself. Tug-of-war with a massive stick followed, after which Ernest had to pee on quite a few things. They soon found themselves nearing the lake where many more people had congregated, drawn by the cafe and high volume of ducks to feed. Mums were crouching next to pushchairs, alternately pointing and offering bread to the ducks, who gathered and splattered around the path, noisily accepting the most recently thrown items.

As Nathan paused, taking it all in and wondering which way they should go around the path, he noticed somebody coming towards him.

"Sausage dog!" cried the child, who Nathan could see now was actually quite near his age, and, even worse, was a girl. Metaphorical thunderclouds bloomed above his head and the heavens opened. He put up his hood and tried to zip his coat, and as he did so, he fumbled the lead, and Ernest took his chance. The heady combination of duck poo and bread was too much for him. He lurched forward, giddy with the possibilities before him, and left Nathan leadless, dogless and helpless.

Luckily for Nathan, the girl was not as bad as he thought she was, and slightly younger than him too. She quickly realised what was happening and spun around to follow the trailing lead and liberated dog. Nathan abandoned his coat rearrangement and ran after her and the dog. His cries of "Ernest! Ernest!" fell on deaf ears, and even the tasty treat bag could not work its usual magic. Ernest ran like a tiny young gazelle, dodging the ducks and going straight to the bread that littered the water's edge. Just as Nathan had reached him and was about to grab the lead, Ernest skipped sideways, catching the trailing lead under the wheel of a pushchair. This upset his balance and that of the pushchair, propelling both dog and pushchair forwards towards the lake.

The fact that the pushchair was empty was good news for the stunned toddler clutching her concerned mother, but bad news for Ernest, as he was now inextricably linked to a free-moving plastic vehicle of about the same weight as him. The pushchair toppled undramatically into the lake, dragging poor Ernest with it. The water was pathetically shallow, 15 cm at most, but it was enough to knock the wind out of Ernest's sails and cause Nathan to leap heroically in to save the embarrassed dog. The water may not have been deep, but what it lacked in depth it more than made up for in odour. It really, really stank, and so did Ernest. Nathan's trainers and the first 10 cm of his trousers were soaked through and streaked with thick black-green muck.

He didn't care, Ernest knew it, and loved him for it. If Nathan had been a god before, now he was a hero too. Nathan clutched the dog to his chest, and slooped out of the lake, watched by an interested crowd of toddlers, parents and the girl. He let Ernest lick his neck, but drew the line at his face (Ew! Duck poo!) and once their heartbeats had slowed down in tandem, he put the little dog on the ground, the better to check him over. The girl stood awkwardly but interestedly by.

"Is she okay?" she asked, shifting her weight to one foot.

"It's a he. I think so," replied Nathan, stroking Ernest.

"What's his name?"

"Ernest."

"Hi Ernest," said the girl, dropping down on to the grass next to him.

Nathan was concentrating on getting the treats bag out and this action immediately proved that Ernest was indeed okay. He smartened into a tidy sit and fixed Nathan with his beautiful adoring brown eyes.

"Can I give him one?" asked the girl.

"Yeah, sure. Here you go," said Nathan, handing over a treat from the bag. She laughed as she made Ernest sit, insisting that he wait until his bottom was actually touching the grass.

"Good dog! What a good boy!" she sang as she smoothed his ears then tickled him under his chin, oblivious to the duck poo.

"You're so lucky," she continued, "sausage dogs are my very favourite dog." She didn't once look at Nathan, just gloried in being so close to her idol.

"Oh, he's not mine, he belongs to...oh, someone else. I'm just walking him. Sorry, I've got to go, I was supposed to be back a while ago. Bye."

That this was officially the longest sentence had ever spoken to girl since he was about eight did not occur to him. He just knew that if he didn't get Ernest back to the model shop within the next ten minutes, he would surely lose the possibility of ever being trusted with him again.

By the time Nathan got back to the shop, Martin and Alan had compiled the bones of a plan. Now that Ernest was clearly Martin's responsibility for at least the next two weeks, he could deal with it more effectively. He could not and would not look further than the fortnight ahead, and he had parked his New Zealand trip in a secure and temporarily inaccessible part of his brain. Alan however was quite animated by the drama, coming as it did on top of the whole Spitfire/Messerschmitt/Titanic excitement, and as Nathan and Ernest beeped in through the door he was almost actively pleased to see them.

"Ah, good, you're back." Stating the obvious came naturally to Alan.

"Yes, we're back," confirmed Nathan, unnecessarily he felt, but sometimes he knew how and when to play the game that kept the adults happy. They clearly *were* back, and so far, the excess six minutes of his trip to the park did not seem to be an issue. In fact, as soon as Nathan flipped back his hood, he felt the eyes of expectation upon him.

The two men exchanged glances and Martin shifted forward slightly on his plinth. "So, did you have a nice time at the park?" he enquired.

Nathan was pretty sure this wasn't a loaded question. Neither of them were looking at his wet trousers, and the off duck poo stench of the dog hadn't had time to warm up and get going yet. He furtively wiped the front of his anorak. He was going to go all-out innocent.

"Yes thank you Mr...er... Martin. I kept him on his lead. He was really good." Two truths and a lie, but the two men seemed to buy it.

"Well, that's good, isn't it Martin?"

Martin agreed that it was good and looked encouragingly at Alan, who continued.

"It looks as if Ernest's going to be with Martin for a bit longer, couple of weeks?" Alan looked for confirmation from Martin.

"Oh, yes, a fortnight, for sure," agreed Martin.

"And we were wondering if you might like a little job?"

Nathan decided to play for time and remained noncommittal. Alan would have to try a little harder. It was like pulling teeth, except for free.

"Martin's going to have Ernest in the shop with him, but he's going to need somebody to take him for a really good walk every day."

Nathan still didn't respond. He wasn't being thick or tricky, it was just that he thought he had been offered the chance to walk Ernest on a daily basis and before he let his heart soar with the angels and joy flood his soul, he wanted to check that was indeed what was being offered. A lot of his reticence to engage came from a fear of exposing his level of understanding of long strings of words that he just couldn't keep up with. Words went in, he knew what they meant, but they weren't always in the right order and sometimes quite big chunks got crushed by the weight of the other words backing up behind them.

"D'you want me to walk Ernest?"

"Yes," said both men at once. Ernest himself followed the words visually, like a Wimbledon enthusiast.

"I can come straight here after school. I finish at 3 o'clock." Inside, champagne corks were popping, bunting had been put up and samba music was playing. Outside, he just smiled and looked at Ernest, who returned his gaze lovingly and sat, hoping for a treat, which he got.

"I'm sure Claire will be fine with it, but I'll ask her this evening and confirm it with you then," Alan said.

"Of course. Must make sure it's okay with 'mum'." Martin directed this at Nathan, and although he did not actually do the air quotes thing that he sometimes did, it was implicit in his delivery. This made no sense to Nathan. She was his mum. However, he mentally shrugged and savoured the future which was bright and involved walking Ernest every day for the next two weeks. He delivered Ernest, the poo bags and the treat bags behind the plinth, and having collected the Titanic and the planes, they left the shop in high spirits.

Alan noticed Nathan's trainers and trousers and smiled to himself. He didn't think he'd ever seen Nathan muddy before. Jackie had always been good about the state of Robert's clothes and he had followed her lead. She saw it as a sign that he'd been having a good time and he didn't remember her ever being cross with the boy about clothes, even when he'd ripped the leg right off his new jeans, falling out of a tree. They had encouraged both children to play outside as much as possible, and they had raced round on bikes with a few others who lived on the close. They had made dens and mud pies in the bit round the back, all overgrown in those days, but now just more neat houses, parking spaces and tidy gardens.

She had been forever putting things in the wash, mending rips, and scrubbing trainers. As they got older, there had been less need for this kind of care, but Alan could picture Jackie now, motionless by the open back door, leaning against the washing machine, a pair of Robert's trainers in her hands. They were grimy and worn, dry mud caking the sides, but she held them with the tenderness of a new mother. Robert wouldn't need them again. The shape of his feet was as near to him as she could get. Gently, she had pulled them to her chest and cried and cried and cried. He'd held her, but he couldn't reach her. So, muddy trainers on a little lad, his own living flesh and bone, gave him the greatest pleasure that he had felt in a long time.

Chapter 14

Claire had already left for work before the boys were even up on Monday morning. She had a presentation to give in Norwich, and rather than take up the company's generous offer of a night in the Premier Inn beforehand, she had chosen to get up early and forfeit breakfast with her boys. People sometimes referred to them as 'the boys', as in "How are the boys?", but to Claire this was not only lazy and implied that the person enquiring didn't actually know their individual names, but it also missed the whole point of their being two separate people. The only thing they shared was parentage and gender.

When Matt was born, she and Carl had been beyond thrilled. They had sat and just looked at him, basking in his perfection, the wonder of his newness, the miracle of his being. Claire clearly remembered Matt lying out in just a nappy on a quilted blanket her mother had bought him, sunlight streaming through the window and catching his duckling hair from the side. His unpracticed fingers had opened and closed in an amateur, experimental way and they had both pointed and held their breath in delight. He had fixed them with his dusty blue eyes and she had reached out to Carl, kneeling next to her on the carpet and looked from him to the baby and back again. She remembered having so much love she didn't know what to do with it, but somehow being unable to share that with Carl. Or was that just with hindsight? Perhaps they had been really happy, really together and it was just now that it was not possible for her fleabitten heart to let her remember that.

Long journeys brought on Claire's retrospective side, allowing her time to look back and wonder in a way her normal daily life did not. Having turned her thoughts to Carl now, she felt herself tense up. It was fresh, it was a raw, it was nearly three years ago, for goodness' sake, surely she should be feeling better than this? When he had left, suddenly, one Wednesday evening whilst Matt and Nathan were at Cubs, it had initially been a huge shock. He'd always had his own things going on; mountain biking, running and skateboarding (really? skateboarding? He was supposed to be a grown-up man) and she had always accepted that his leisure time was going to include a lot of hours doing these things that she didn't share. She had no idea that this leisure time had also included Nicola. Nicola, her ex-friend, who ironically and unwittingly on Claire's part, had actually been a shared interest. They'd got to know each other when Nathan was at nursery and they had similar work schedules, picking up their kids at the same time, chatting about mum stuff. When Claire realised that Nicola was on her own with Nancy, she had done what she could to reach out and help, and a friendship of sorts had developed. Nicola was a keen runner but finding someone to have Nancy was tricky, and Claire had been happy to include the little girl in her weekend plans from time to time and of course, Carl was a keen runner too. She should have seen it coming, but really, what with work and then her mother dying, she had just been in survival mode. He hadn't left because of Nicola. That had been discovered, admitted to, and accepted as a leisure interest that had passed and been forgiven. They had cobbled it together, not really for the sake of the children, but because Claire really loved him and so, when he announced that he was leaving her for some woman he'd met through mountain biking she didn't have the energy to fall apart, she just helped him pack.

Her mother's death, when Nathan had just turned two, seemed buried now in holding it together for two small children, holding down a demanding job in a male-dominated competitive environment and holding onto her sanity. She didn't really have memories of the time, just facts and photographs. She did, however, remember expressing to the night sky - alone in the back garden one night, tears of rage streaming down her cheeks - that the wrong parent had died, and whilst even thinking about this made her stomach flip over with unexpressed guilt, there were times that she still believed this. Her dad was okay, he was there, but he wasn't her mum, in so many ways. Claire had had to grow up fast after Robert died, and besides the grief, the halting of everything, she had ached to be a normal teenager who didn't live in a house stalled by loss and shadows. She had channelled her guilt at being alive into working hard at school and her successful career in pharmaceutical sales reflected this. She was also extremely thorough, paid attention to detail and researched everything she ever did to within an inch of her life.

Just like Alan.

*

She decided to give him a quick ring now and briefly diced with danger by pressing buttons on her 'hands-free' mobile, whilst cursing the fact that Tony, who was on the same level in her company, had a fancy system in his car that was voice-activated. She'd never thought to bargain for this upgrade and instead maintained the Audi she had since Matt was born, too busy actually doing the job to negotiate her own terms. Her father answered on the second ring, giving his full phone number, including area code, like it was still 1987.

"Dad, hi," she began.

"Who is this please?" Alan interrupted.

"It's me, Dad, it's Claire."

"Oh, Claire, hello, it's a terrible line. Can you hear me?"

"Yes, Dad, I can hear you. Can you hear me?"

They did this routine on most phone calls.

"Yes, I can now, but it's not a very good line."

"Everything okay?"

"Yes, all good. Just checking you're okay to have Nathan after school?"

"Yes, he's coming here with the dog. What time do you think you'll be back?" He was wondering about supper, and if that mince from the butcher would still be okay to use.

"Well, I'm hoping to be done by four, but then we've got a team meeting and it'll be a good two hours back, with the traffic then."

"Mmm, are you thinking to cut through on the 414 when you come off the A1?" Alan mused, "It'll probably save you about 20 minutes if you're coming southbound, that time of day."

"Thanks Dad," said Claire, trying to sound sincere, but not too interested, in case it set him off on his M25 theories, "would you be okay to give Nathan his supper?"

"Absolutely, spag bol all round! What about Matt?"

"Oh, he'll do his own thing. He's got hockey straight after school, then he's going to Caleb's. Some project? He said they've offered to give him tea, but I've told him to be home by nine. I should be long back by then."

"Okay, I'll walk with Nathan to take the dog back, then you pick him up from here on your way home. Okay? Give us a bit of Titanic Time."

Claire registered the phrase as slightly odd but chose not to pick up on it.

"Yes, good, thanks Dad, I've got to go, another call coming in. Thanks, bye."

Claire's mind was already on to sales figures and the possibility of the pop up banner she needed having been sent to the Nantwich office, rather than the Norwich office to which she was currently heading, for pity's sake.

Alan meanwhile, went straight to the fridge to sniff the mince. He ripped open the thin white plastic bag and inhaled deeply. Ripe, meaty, but not off. Good. He went on to spend a happy day constructing a confident spaghetti bolognese and preparing the dining room table for 'Titanic Time', scheduled to begin at approximately 4.45.

Chapter 15

The first few days of dog walking went without a hitch. Nathan clock-watched his way through school, barely noticing that he had been moved up a set for maths, and then, as soon as the bell went, he left as quickly as he could without drawing attention to himself. Ernest was beside himself to see Nathan each day. Martin was surprised to find that behind the relief he expected at having the dog out of his hair for a while lay some pleasant anticipation of the boy's arrival.

Martin had looked out some fairly recent issues of *Fine Scale Modeller*, carefully marking articles he thought Nathan might benefit from with labelled post-its. It being quiet in the shop, he began looking through the January 2016 edition, which he remembered, correctly, contained an article about how to improve the build on Monogram's F-14, a model he was thinking about recommending for Nathan's next project. The *Top Gun* connection might prove appealing and everybody loves a Tomcat. Whilst browsing the magazine, he had come across an article about a father and son building a 1/35 scale Sherman Tank. He did not particularly rate the manufacturer, Tamiya not being a brand he stocked, but he thought Alan might be interested in some of the tips for engaging youngsters with model making. He wondered if he should offer to teach Nathan how to airbrush his models, as he knew Alan did not have his own airbrush. Previously this had given him a frisson of satisfaction, but now he was starting to think of how good it might feel to share not only his equipment (under close supervision of course) but perhaps some of his knowledge too. Being unused to children, Martin made notes from the article, taking on board unsettling phrases like 'try to resist redoing the kid's work,' and 'don't be frustrated if your youngster doesn't get it right at first.' He resolved to give Nathan (for free), a Prismacolor pencil when he came in to fetch Ernest later. He imagined explaining to the rapt boy how it would help him to accentuate detail on his build, the boy then leaving with the pencil held aloft like the Holy Grail.

Nathan pinged into the shop just after 3.10 and Ernest, who had been pacing and whistling simultaneously since 3.05 leapt to the end of his lead to greet him. Nathan dropped to the ground, his rucksack skittering to a halt at the plinth edge as he discarded it the better to embrace Ernest.

Martin looked on fondly from his slightly elevated position.

"How's The Titanic going Nathan?"

"Yeah, good, pretty much got all the parts out of the sprue tree now."

Martin felt oddly emotional to hear him using the phrase 'sprue tree.' He had fully expected him to say something like 'plastic frame' or 'bit that holds the parts,' but Nathan's use of the correct word for the specific item made him feel warm and hopeful for the future of model making.

"Has your grandad said anything about painting yet?"

"Well, some parts are pre-painted, which he's not happy about, but all the paints are in there."

"Mmm, has he said anything about airbrushing it?"

"No...." Nathan tailed off, distracted by the frantic attentions of Ernest.

"Well, most modellers agree that a superior finish can be obtained with airbrushing, and I would be happy to instruct you in the art, using my own equipment." It was a far bigger offer than the Prismacolor pencil he had envisaged, but it was out there now. He rocked back on his heels, waiting for the flood of gratitude he expected this speech to illicit. It was not forthcoming.

"Erm, maybe. Think I've got to get going now, Ernest's going mental! See you later Mr, er, Martin," and with a reverse ping, he left the shop, leaving Martin wondering.

Ernest and Nathan had a great time at the park and even though the day was fine and bright, there were very few other people and dogs around. Nathan had begun to be a little weary of Ernest's constant pulling on the lead, and had made some headway with training him to walk more sensibly to heel. Nathan decided that the time had come to try some off-lead work. He had plenty of treats and also a sausage that he had reserved from his lunch. He chose the most remote bit of the park, well away from the road, and unclipping the little dog from his lead began to establish recall. It was extremely easy, as once Ernest knew there was actual sausage on offer, he didn't move more than 30 cm away from him. Nathan began to run and play in the leaves, focusing fully on the dog, noting his reactions and setting him up to succeed, just as he'd researched on the Internet. So focused was he that he didn't notice he was being watched.

As soon as the girl saw him, she started to run towards him, leaving her brother deep in his phone and still trudging along the path.

"Ernest!!" she called, her blonde hair bouncing happily behind her as she ran through the leaves.

Ernest and Nathan saw her at the same time, but had very different reactions.

Nathan hurriedly fumbled to clip Ernest's lead on, hoping to avoid a repeat of their last meeting, or indeed any meeting, but as usual, Ernest got his own way. Ears streaming behind him, he launched himself at the girl, making an open and heartfelt greeting his top priority. She knelt immediately to make contact with his hot sleek body, giving him many compliments and agreeing with whatever it was his body language was saying.

Nathan sat down as well, having no choice but to join in and adore Ernest too; however, he did manage to put the lead on before anything else happened.

"I'm so happy to see you Ernest," explained the girl unnecessarily. Nathan knew that feeling though, and began to build a small rickety bridge of communication between him and this girl.

"He's just learning recall?" he ventured, allowing her space, if she needed it, to ask what recall was. She didn't.

"Oh wow! That's so great. I saw this video on YouTube where they used bits of sausage. The dogs were going mad for it! Apparently it's a high value treat."

"Yes!" Nathan pulled the slightly careworn sausage from his anorak pocket and they laughed as Ernest instantly hovered his haunches over the damp grass in his best imitation of a 'sit'.

Now that the ice was broken, the girl introduced herself as Daisy and Nathan introduced himself as Nathan. They were just starting to set up a system whereby Ernest would rush from one of them to the other, when they were interrupted by a dark-haired boy, back lit by the lowering evening sun.

"Daisy, come on, we have to go."

"Oh, yes, sorry. Nathan, this is my brother Troy."

"Hi."

"Hi."

Nathan checked his watch in the ensuing awkwardness and realised that he had to go too. He had arranged with Grandad that he would take Ernest back to the shop today, and the shop closed at 5 o'clock but Martin had asked him to be back at 4.45 to allow for something that he hadn't listened to but understood to be important. Possibly something to do with keys? Or alarms?

Gathering his thoughts and 'his' dog, he started to head off in the direction of the shop without a backward glance. It soon became apparent that Daisy and this Troy person were following him, albeit at a distance. At every road crossing and turn, he furtively checked to see if they had stopped following, but they kept on coming. He was relieved to ping into the shop and shut the door firmly behind him. Only seconds later, the door pinged open and his pursuers stepped inside.

Martin didn't bat an eyelid.

"Afternoon, Troy. I see you've met Nathan."

The two boys looked at one another briefly, then bizarrely Nathan blushed a deep scarlet.

"Yes, Nathan's in my maths set now," piped up Troy. Of course he

71

was! Nathan realised that he had actually been sitting at the next desk to this boy today, and he had actually had quite a good conversation about algebraic techniques, also today, and now this boy would think he had blanked him and that was bad because he had never been able to have a good conversation about algebraic techniques with anyone before and it had felt great and now it would never happen again because he had failed to .....

Daisy broke the negative spiral of thoughts in his head by saying brightly

"Oh cool! So you know each other already! Nathan's dog Ernest is the best! Aren't you Ernest?"

Everybody looked at Ernest. He agreed.

Martin greased the wheels of conversation by explaining exactly whose dog Ernest was, and how the general arrangements had come about, and then caught sight of the time.

"Anyway Troy, how can I help you today?"

Troy and Martin launched into a complex conversation about the best type of pin vice and if an adjustable chuck collet was either necessary or desirable. Nathan listened surreptitiously to the conversation whilst rubbing Ernest's ears, but once Martin got out the two pin vices that he stocked for Troy to have a look at, he gave in to his curiosity and joined them at the plinth. Troy's pre-teen hands were smaller than those that the first pin vice had been designed for and Martin steered him towards the marginally more expensive but slightly more slender-handled version that would better suit his needs.

Nathan threw caution to the wind.

"What's it for?" he breathed.

Troy was happy to explain that it could be used to hold small parts still for operations like sanding and thus was a vital part of the model maker's kit.

"Is this a cash purchase, or will you be putting it on 'dad's' account?"

It seemed that putting parents' names into inverted commas

came naturally to Martin, and Nathan and Troy exchanged an almost imperceptible acknowledgement that this was a weird thing to do.

"Yes please, on my dad's account. He said we can't get on until I have one I can use properly."

"Ah yes, the big project!"

Turning to Nathan, Martin carried on, "Troy and his 'dad'" (Nathan and Troy made definite eye contact) "are preparing for the nationals. Not long to go now, eh Troy?"

"Yeah, it's the beginning of November."

"Still in Telford?"

"Yes, every year now."

Martin turned to Nathan.

"You are looking at the 'son' of the winner of the silver medal in class 1 of the Aircraft category at Scale ModelWorld 17, am I right Troy?"

Troy glance briefly at Nathan before replying.

"Yes, that is correct, he is my 'dad' and he did indeed win the silver medal in that class," Troy confirmed, having the presence of mind and sheer guts to make actual air quotes around the word dad, "and this year he's hoping for gold."

Nathan was blown away, on so many levels. Martin didn't notice, Daisy wasn't listening and Ernest didn't care.

"And are you entering any junior classes this year Troy?"

"I think so, we think my tank model would be the one to enter. If I can just get the finish right I think I'm in with a chance."

"I'd love to see it when it's done. I bet Nathan would too. He's just starting out, but his first project was most promising. Can't remember when I saw a nicer pair from the Dogfight Doubles series."

"I've made some of those! Messerschmitt and Mustang?"

"No, Messerschmitt and Spitfire. But I've just started on the Titanic."

"No way! I did that last year, I got it for my birthday!"

Chapter 16

Over the next week or so, everyone settled into a routine. Troy and Nathan spent time together, with and without Ernest and Daisy, and their respective modelling projects benefited from the collaboration. Troy dragged Nathan along to the school Model Club, run by Mr Peterson, his chemistry teacher and Martin's near neighbour. This fact had put him off joining before, but Troy reassured him that all would be well. Nathan was shocked at how different Mr Peterson was at Model Club, and he and Troy decided that their chemistry teacher was in fact this Mr Peterson's evil twin.

Claire became properly aware of what 'Titanic Time' was, and looked fondly on as her dad and her son bent over the dining table, united in a shared interest. She knew that Alan had always been interested in this sort of thing, but neither she nor Robert had felt it was something that could have included them. It had just been 'Dad's thing' and she certainly never remembered him talking about, let alone showing them, what he was up to. If she remembered anything, it was a certain possessiveness, perhaps a private activity that gave him a place to retreat to? She had a memory of her mother being rather scathing of the hobby, referring to his 'toys' and making him tidy it away, until there hadn't been a mental or physical space for it in the house. What he had done in his shed was of no interest to his family, and looking at him now with Nathan, Claire felt a certain sense of shame.

However, coming in from work to see the two of them sharing tools, ideas and skills gave her great contentment, a feeling that had long been missing in her life. She had her own key, so she didn't have to disturb them, but Ernest now included her in his list of adored people and she got the full welcome if he was at the house, which he often was. She had never had a dog, not through dislike, but really through ambivalence. She had enough going on, and although Nathan in particular had always said how much he wanted a dog, she had found it easy to say no. She didn't like the way Ernest scrabbled at her tights, but Nathan had taught her how to get Ernest to sit, which he usually did now, and it was a step in the right direction towards pleasant relations between them.

Nathan had told her all about his new friend Troy, and she had met him and thought he seemed very nice. She was relieved that Nathan was making friends and when he told her that Troy had said he should come along to after-school model making club, she had made it easy for him to go, by asking Alan to walk the dog that day. Alan was happy to help and made sure he had everything ready for tea before he left to go to the shop.

When he arrived, Martin was rather distracted. He had a lot of paperwork set out on the counter and his laptop was open and to hand. Ernest was sunbathing in the window, an arrangement he had insisted upon, and Martin had facilitated by moving some boxes and altering the display he had set up about eighteen months previously. People had begun to notice the sleeping dog in the window, and unbeknown to Martin, pre-school children were insisting that their walks and pushchair rides came past 'the dog shop' on the way to the park.

Ernest raised his head at the ping of the door, and lazily thumped his tail several times, the canine equivalent of the courteous nod of greeting which Alan gave him in return.

"Martin, Ernest," Alan said pleasantly.

"Afternoon Alan. I'm afraid I can't offer you coffee as I have too many arrangements to make and I'm waiting for a call back from my insurers." He continued to shuffle papers and look between his laptop and phone.

"No problem. I could make one for both of us if you'd like?'

Martin looked up and over his reading glasses, stunned briefly by this revelatory idea. Somebody else make a hot drink in his shop? It hadn't been done before, but, yes, why not?

"Thank you Alan, that would be most welcome. You will find everything you need in the area to my left, just at the rear there. One spoon of coffee, splash of cold water, boiling water in, splash of milk, one of sugar and I'm the IPMS UK mug." He hoped it wasn't too obvious that he didn't trust Alan, but he didn't. He couldn't help it, and it wasn't because of anything Alan had done or not done. It was about liking his coffee like he liked his coffee, in a mug he liked. He tried to immerse himself in the insurance paperwork, and by the time Alan appeared with two mugs of coffee, he made a good show of being grateful. The mug was correct, the coffee was drinkable and Alan seemed quite pleased with himself.

"What's the issue with the insurer?" Alan, asked, nodding towards the piles of paper.

Martin took a deep breath, in for five, and exhaled for seven. He'd seen a feature on breakfast television about managing stress and found this technique most helpful. Better. He wasn't sure where exactly to start, so he just came out with it.

"I'm going to New Zealand in two weeks' time."

Alan couldn't tell if this was a good thing, a bad thing or just a thing. He remained quiet, blowing on his coffee, waiting for more information.

Martin did another in for five, out for seven then related to Alan the whole story - Gerry, their rekindled friendship, the passing of time, the taking of opportunities, diminishing customer sales and footfall. Obviously they were not disturbed by any customers, and Alan was able to fully understand the situation within ten minutes or so. He had to have some clarification about Gerry, as he did remember him, but wasn't sure of his surname and initially thought it was Gerry Thomas, who'd had The Cross Keys pub and gone to New Zealand too, but actually he hadn't, he'd gone to Spain, and it was more to do with a misunderstanding over the brewery accounts than a lifestyle opportunity.

"So there it is. The shop will have to close for the duration of my absence, that much is decided, but I need to clear it with my insurers. What is not so clear-cut is what to do about Ernest. I heard no more from that Judy person and she's not answering my calls."

They both looked at the dog, flat out in the window, oblivious to everything.

"What's the news on Joan?'

"The operation was a success, and they're moving her to a nursing home tomorrow. There's no way she can go back home, she just wouldn't manage. I shall have to go in and arrange about her possessions, and terminate the lease with the landlord, but her neighbour, Carol, has said that she will help with that side of things."

"What does Joan say about Ernest?"

"Well, she asks about him, every time I see her, but she's not as sharp as she was, and I think she thinks that Sheila's looking after him."

Both men looked firmly at their coffees. Sheila would indeed have looked after Ernest, and done it with a spring in her step too. Martin was looking after Ernest, and he wasn't hating it, now that they had firm boundaries in place (Martin would not allow Ernest on the furniture, Ernest would not sleep anywhere else but in Martin's bed) and the support of Nathan and Alan, but it was a duty, not a joy.

They were saved from further introspection by Martin's phone - it was the insurance company. They were happy for the shop to be closed for a five-week period, but it would incur a significantly higher premium. Martin waited patiently on hold while the calculations were made, holding his credit card with his free hand, really to read the numbers out and pay. The hold music stopped abruptly.

"Mr Rundle? Thank you for holding. There is indeed an additional premium payable by yourself. Are you happy to make that payment today?"

Martin said that he was, but when she said the amount he knew that he could not pay today, or indeed any other day. The shop finances simply couldn't sustain that kind of figure. Weakly he asked her to repeat the amount to be sure he had it right, thanked the lady and said that he would have to call her back. It was New Zealand or the shop.

Chapter 17

Martin's news got everybody thinking, and by the time Alan, Nathan and Claire sat down to a meal a day or so later, there was plenty to talk about. It was jacket potatoes, with the very last of the spag bol (frozen, defrosted and re-invented as chilli con carne with the addition of a tin of kidney beans and some mild chilli powder.) Alan couldn't stand waste and had been a closet fan of *Ready, Steady, Cook!* even when Jackie had been alive. He tried to use every last item in his fridge before replenishing stores and this meal had made use of a sad pepper, two spring onions and a rogue radish that would otherwise have gone to compost. Not all his efforts to creatively use random ingredients turned out so well, but this one was good.

"This is really good Grandad. Can you do this again when Troy comes next week?" Nathan said through a large mouthful.

"Well, I may not be able to recreate the exact recipe but I'll give it my best shot. I'm just sorry Matt isn't here to have some."

"I know," agreed Claire, "but I'm glad he's doing this play at school. It makes a change from hockey and he's meeting a different crowd."

"You didn't fancy the school play then, Nathan?" said Alan, turning to his grandson with a wry look.

"Very funny Grandad," he replied, as clearly as the potato allowed. Claire looked between them, trying to make sense of the dynamic. It looked like light-hearted banter. Could it be light-hearted banter? Based on her previous experience of their relationship it seemed unlikely, but her interest was piqued.

Ernest huffed under the table. Nobody had noticed him for over ten minutes and it was time to address that.

"What time are you taking the dog back Nathan? It's starting to get dark."

Ernest was staying a little later than usual so Martin could visit Joan in the nursing home. Martin was keen to see her settled so that he could try and make a decision about New Zealand.

"I'm going just now. That was a nice tea, thanks Grandad."

Claire looked up, resting her knife and fork on the side of her plate. "D'you want me to come with you? It'll be properly dark by the time you get back."

"Mum! I'm twelve! I'll be fine!"

"Boy's right Claire, it's not exactly far and it's all street lights. He'll be fine." He looked warmly at Nathan, who was already putting the dog's lead on.

"I'll be back in 20 minutes, see you!" and with a zip of his anorak, he was gone.

*

Claire waited until the door had shut behind him, then sighed and said, "What's going to happen when that dog has to go, I wonder? Martin won't want to keep him permanently, and if he does go to New Zealand, he'll have to make a decision pretty soon. Nathan's going to be heartbroken."

"Yes. About that. I've been thinking."

Alan had indeed been thinking. He had been unable to settle at bedtime and woken unusually early for the past few days, and even tidying his shed had failed to sooth his busy mind. Eventually he had taken a pad of lined A4 paper, carefully removed two sheets and put them side-by-side on the dining room table. He had headed one sheet 'shop' and one sheet 'dog.' He fetched these papers now and put them beside Claire at the table. This was standard practice, and Claire began to read immediately, knowing that a response would not be forthcoming from Alan until she had read and digested the information he had given her. This was a method that had been introduced during Claire's teenage years and been used by both of them to prove maturity (Claire) and avoid confrontation (Alan). Jackie had initially teased them both lightly, but quickly realised that it worked for them and made for a peaceful home life. Claire had been able to go to the university of her choice and Alan had been able to show that although her travel costs to and from home would be higher if she studied further away, by choosing a city served by a direct National Express route, this could be mitigated.

Claire finally looked up at Alan's expectant face.

"Good plan, Dad."

"Thank you. As you can see, there will be some costs involved, but I'm pretty confident that once I've spoken to Martin, we can work something out."

"Haven't you spoken to him yet?'

"Not as yet, but I think I have covered every eventuality, so I don't foresee him being anything other than agreeable."

"Don't say anything to Nathan yet though, just in case?"

Alan looked surprised. "That's implicit in point eleven, page two, I would have thought."

Claire looked again.

"Sorry Dad. Yes, of course. Long day."

"Long day. Cup of tea?"

Chapter 18

By almost close of business next day, it was sorted. Martin had of course leapt at Alan's offer to take on Ernest full time and forever. There had never been any doubt about that. The custodianship of the shop had been a slightly more involved decision, but Martin could see the sense in Alan keeping everything ticking over, and he was, quite frankly, impressed at the attention to detail he saw in the six page document Alan handed him. There was literally nothing that Alan had not thought of. Both men stood on the plinth and leant over the counter together, Martin filling in the blank sections of Alan's itinerary. Bin day had been something that Alan had had to leave blank, living as he did in a different part of town, but the principles of black bin, purple bin and brown box were all the same of course. He had thought that business collection might be slightly different to residential, but had been reassured that the colours were the same even though the days and sizes of bins were different. Martin was able to show him a lever arch folder devoted to refuse collection and Alan felt hugely reassured that such a folder existed. In fact, there were folders for pretty much any eventuality. Colour coded, date ordered and neatly shelved, in an alcove to the rear and right of the plinth.

An air of satisfaction and mutual admiration hung above the plinth, bathing both the men in contentment and wellbeing. Point 14, page 2, outlined arrangements that needed to be made about Ernest visiting Joan in the nursing home, and it was this point that was being considered when Nathan came pinging in the door, just after three.

"Ah, Nathan," ventured Martin, whilst Alan stepped around the plinth to the shop side, a little awkwardly. He hadn't mentioned any of the plans to Nathan, and he wanted to get it right.

"Hello, Mr, er Martin, hi Grandad. Is Ernest ready for his walk?"

This last comment was directed directly at Ernest who had been shifting from foot to foot by the door for sometime.

"I'll just get his lead, shall I?" Nathan could sense that something was up, but he made a resolute decision to ignore it and concentrate on Ernest. However, he was thwarted at the plinth. Martin stepped sideways, blocking his access to the lead.

"So, Nathan, I know how much you enjoy walking Ernest, but there are going to be a few changes from now on."

Nathan stopped breathing. He felt all his blood contract into the cavities behind his eyes. Time stopped too; motes of dust caught in the weak afternoon sun paused in mid-air. This was the thing that he had dreaded, the talk where he found out that Ernest was going back to his owner, or perhaps the elusive Judy Something.

Ernest barked sharply, breaking the poignancy of the moment.

"Changes? Like what?' Nathan needed clarification and he wasn't afraid to ask.

"Well, as you know, his owner, Joan, had a nasty fall. Her hip is mending but she's not physically strong enough to manage at home any more, let alone manage a dog like Ernest." He paused and they all turned to look at Ernest, who had his back turned against them all and was furiously licking his bits.

"She's gone into a home, you might know it, Foxholes? It's on the road that goes out past Sainsbury's? Linden Road?"

Nathan looked blank, but Martin soldiered on.

"Used to be a big private house, portico over the door, driveway with a hedge?"

Nothing from Nathan.

"It's got a big maroon sign outside, saying 'Foxholes' in large gold letters, but actually they had to take it down last week,… again, as some wag had vandalised the sign… again. I don't know why they don't just change the name. Once people have thought of it as Arseholes, the damage is done."

Alan stepped in at this point. He could stand it no longer.

"What Martin is trying to say is, would we like to have Ernest permanently?"

Relief flooded through Nathan and he dropped down to the floor to be nearer Ernest's level. He didn't need words, but just in case there was any doubt, he exclaimed, "Yes, yes, yes, we would. Wouldn't we Ernest? Oh, yes, what a good dog, who's a good dog? You are, oh yes!"

He fluffed Ernest's ears and then smoothed them, encouraging the little dog to stand on his waiting lap and get as close to him as possible.

"There are one or two conditions, Nathan," explained Martin.

Nathan looked up, but carried on holding on to Ernest.

"Yes, we think, your grandad and I, that it would only be right for you to take Ernest to see Joan at Foxholes a couple of times a week. She's certainly not as sharp as she was, but I think it would do her the world of good to see that dog."

Nathan got that. Of course Ernest would do you good.

"I can do that." He paused. "But will he actually be my dog, or her dog still?"

"In the eyes of the world, he will be your dog, but it may be that Joan will still think of him as her dog, and treat you as if you are looking after him for her. So, when you are at Foxholes, maybe he's Joan's dog, but everywhere else, he will be your dog. Your dog, Nathan. Okay?"

"Yeah, I get it Grandad, I get it. I can do that."

"And I will help you with him, and look after him when you are at school, but he will be your dog. I've spoken to mum, and she is okay with everything."

"Oh, yes, must make sure 'mum' is on board. Very important," agreed Martin.

Even Alan couldn't let that one go. He looked meaningfully at Nathan, who bravely remained straight-faced.

"So, Nathan, are you going to take your dog for a walk, or not?"

Nathan smiled, properly and with pure joy.

"Yeah, I'll just get his lead. Excuse me, Mr, er Martin."

"And tomorrow, after school, when you fetch him from the shop, you can take him on to see Joan at Foxholes. I've told them to expect you."

"Yeah, fine, can I take Troy with me?" The two boys had already agreed to walk Ernest together and were looking forward to discussing their modelling projects.

Martin and Alan checked in with each other visually. Martin seemed fine with this. Alan seemed fine with this.

"Troy is a nice polite young man, that shouldn't be a problem."

"I don't see why not," agreed Martin.

Nathan was not entirely clear if this meant yes or no. He waited and looked expectantly at his grandfather. He knew that Martin was never going to give him a straight answer. Alan, who was getting so much better at tuning in to Nathan's needs, jolted into life.

'Yes. You can bring Troy." He nodded and smiled broadly to reinforce his message, but Nathan was already out of the door, calling his goodbye over the beeping of the door.

"Well," began Martin, "that went well."

"Yes indeed," replied Alan, "yes indeed."

Chapter 19

Foxholes was to Ernest as a sweetie shop is to a toddler. He couldn't believe that there were so many opportunities in one place. He was immediately entranced by the tea trolley, which just so happened to be passing in the foyer as Nathan and Troy arrived. They had been buzzed in remotely, and to be met by, effectively, a giant packet of biscuits on wheels seemed both magical and dreamlike. Ernest was immediately enthralled, and lunged towards the now receding trolley, lugging the boys in his determined wake.

"Oh bless him, does he want a biscuit?" the lady pushing the trolley cooed as she caught sight of Ernest. Ernest pleaded with every fibre of his being, wagging stiffly and ferociously to indicate, he hoped, a clear yes.

"I guess. If that's okay with you. But make him sit first. He can, if you say sit."

"Oh, he's so cute. What's his name?"

*

And so it began. Every person they met on the way to Joan's room had to go through the same procedure, to the extent that Troy and Nathan had to stop and agree to take turns doing the chat. Eventually, they got to Joan's room, assisted by a member of staff called Shirley who was 'a big dog fan'. She started to tell the boys all about her dog Chester, but once Ernest had caught sight of Joan and Nathan took him off his lead, nobody wanted to do anything except focus on the reunion.

Joan had been quietly dozing in bed, roused slightly by Shirley's gentle knock, and to see her face go from sleep to pure contentment, via confusion, recognition, joy, and - briefly - searing pain as Ernest leapt onto her frail body, was an education in the healing power of dogs. Shirley was openly weeping now and inadvertently pressed the call button as she ferreted for her tissue, and so two more staff members were able to witness the scene unfolding. One of them was the kindly lady with the tea trolley, which she had left skewed in the corridor.

Everybody was thrilled with Ernest, and there was a lot of accompanying chatter and questions. The lady in the room next door, who thrived on drama and furtive Werther's originals, lurked outside the door until she saw the dog then openly broke cover and became another fan of Ernest.

Ernest should at this point have snuggled into Joan's crooked elbow, yawned and fallen asleep, but he had better things to do.

"Oh bless," said the lady with the tea trolley for the sixth or seventh time, then added, "Oh well, better get on. Tea, Joan? While I'm here?" turning as she did towards the abandoned trolley. Ernest took a flying leap off the bed and followed her intently.

"Oh bless," she said, "does he want another biscuit?" She didn't really need an answer, and everybody looked on fondly as Ernest necked another custard cream.

She brought Joan's tea, made some more blessings and set off. Ernest, without a backward glance, set off after.

*

This became the pattern for future visits to Foxholes. Sometimes, Ernest was able to add in a bag search, as the residents were very prone to leaving their handbags 'unattended' and Ernest thought nothing of rifling through the handbags of the unaware, the sleeping or even, on one awkward occasion, the dead. He had great success with bins too, managing on a single visit to consume the better part of a banana skin and a used corn plaster before being wrestled to the ground by Nathan. Joan insisted that he didn't need to be on his lead in the home as security was very tight and it was impossible to get anywhere outside without a code, a fob and a buzzer, none of which Ernest had access to.

However, Ernest played the system for all he was worth. His

visits usually coincided with teatime, and he saw it as partially a good walk, and partially his duty to go with the kindly tea trolley lady on her rounds. He developed a special perky walk to accompany the trolley, and it became known to all as his 'biscuit walk.' It was high stepping, efficient and proud, clearly bearing the hallmarks of his German ancestry. It expected reward and it got it. Not only did Kindly Tea Trolley Lady give him a sneaky biscuit as soon as she saw him, but in every resident's room that they visited, the person being given tea would melt and share their biscuits with a good little dog who sat so nicely by their slippered feet. Only occasionally, if Ernest felt they were taking too long to break the biscuit in half (for which there was no need, he could quite easily manage a whole biscuit in one go), their trembling fingers lacking the easy strength of their youth, he would bark sharply, hoping to hurry it all along.

"Oh bless," the person would say, all smiles and indulgence, whilst Ernest fidgeted with impatience.

Sometimes Troy came too, and the two boys were soon known to most of the residents. Neither of them had really come across properly old people before, putting everyone over the age of about twenty into the general category of 'old,' but once they got over the institutional smell of the place, they were fascinated by the diversity and limitations that are part and parcel of old age.

Joan was very pleasant to them, and thanked them profusely and often for bringing Ernest to see her. She also gave them 20p every time they did. The boys found this embarrassing but nice. It allowed to the boys to buy... very little indeed, but as Troy pointed out to Nathan on the walk home, if it kept being offered on a regular basis it could possibly accumulate into the purchase of a bag of crisps and a drink each.

Sometimes Nathan would sit with Joan and Ernest would actually curl up and relax, wedged up against Joan's bony shoulder and building static on her bed jacket.

Sometimes Nathan did his homework whilst Ernest ranged about hoovering up affection and biscuits in equal measure. Sometimes, he would have to go and look for Ernest, creeping quietly from the room so as not to disturb Joan, watching her sleeping breath gently lifting her birdlike chest as he tiptoed out. It was on one of these missions that he found the dayroom, a large communal space near the nurses' station where it was always possible to smell what the last meal had been. Shepherd's Pie, guessed Nathan, something of a mince-based meals expert. A quick glance at the A4 printed menu sheet by the door confirmed this. Nathan paused to look more closely. No apostrophe, he noted. His written English work lacked style and imagination, but his grammar and punctuation were shit hot. He looked around for a marker pen to correct the omission and spotting one on a nearby table, he added the apostrophe carefully.

So absorbed was he in this pedantic task that he did not hear the stealthy swirl of a wheelchair, nor expect the swish of the walking stick that whipped in front of his face and knocked the pen clean out of his hand.

"Got you! I saw you, defacing that menu. Nurse!" she yelled. "Come quickly! Don't think you can talk your way out of this. I know who you are, you're the Arseholer. I'll give you arsehole. Arsehole! Arsehole! Arsehole!"

To Nathan's utter horror she continued to shout "arsehole", flailing her stick at him until a flat-footed but concerned care worker came to his aid.

"Alright, alright, Mrs Bede, it's alright. Hey, hey, now, come on now my darlin'," she soothed. She expertly removed the stick with which Mrs B had effectively been holding the terrified boy captive and span the wheelchair around and away from Nathan. This clearly was not her first rodeo.

Her wealth of experience shone through as she quickly ascertained the situation, talking Mrs B down whilst simultaneously reassuring Nathan and generally pouring oil on troubled waters. It was not long before all parties were clear on all the facts. Nathan had not been defacing the menu, he had merely been adding much needed punctuation, something they should collectively as residents - but especially Mrs B, retired English teacher - be very grateful for. Nathan was the nice boy who brought the dear little dog to see Joan in room 14 and not the horrid person who kept vandalising the sign. Mrs Bede was not a crazed psychopathic killer bent on abusing defenceless grammar-obsessed children, merely a resident whose room looked directly on to the newly 'arseholed' sign, provoked into rage and violence by events beyond her control.

Everybody was given a drink and a biscuit, which helpfully brought Ernest out of the woodwork (actually out of the dayroom bin - an apple core, a juice carton and some tissues, result.)

Nathan couldn't quite bring himself to feel that this had all been Ernest's fault, but he came pretty close.

Chapter 20

Martin had been making pre-flight checks since the moment he and Alan had reached their agreement over the shop and the dog. Time had marched slowly on, and now it was only a matter of days before his departure.

He had reached a point where there was nothing left to say about any aspect of his absence. He knew this, and Alan knew this and they both found it increasingly agitating. Alan was literally counting the hours until Martin's departure; he was ready for solo running of the shop in every way. He had been introduced, by phone, to all the suppliers and long-standing customers. He had been escorted through every lever arch folder and dossier wallet in the shop. He had an intimate knowledge of emergency evacuation plans and had even applied for a special permit at the local tip, in case there was a problem with rubbish collection and he had to take anything from the shop that was too big to fit in his car and would need to go in his trailer.

Martin tremendously appreciated all that Alan had done and would do, but was beginning to feel like a bit of a spare part. He knew Alan knew everything. He knew he had already told him everything, and yet...

He couldn't shake the feeling that he had left some stone unturned. His suitcase was packed and had been for ten days. His passport and tickets were in the safe upstairs. He had decided to renew his passport early, having worried that although the requirement was for the passport to be valid for three months from the date he intended to depart, he would be happier with a full ten years' worth of validity. It had cost him financially but when he weighed up the mental cost of only having four years left on his passport, the benefits of the peace of mind he would gain were certainly greater than the fee involved. He had thought he might need a visa, but Gerry had talked it all through with him over a series of emails, and everything was now in place and ready to go.

He sat at his computer, researching again places of interest near to Gerry's house, and further away too, bearing in mind he had a hire car to use. The screen showed tourist shots of majestic mountains soaring above endless glassy lakes, bordered by open roads and more scenery. Scrolling on, the focus seemed to be on a range of dangerous activities you could do in the aforementioned scenery. Bungee jumping was never going to be on Martin's bucket list. Of course, he didn't actually have a bucket list, but he'd heard it used as a phrase and thought it sounded rather silly. The idea of deliberately seeking out danger and then paying for it seemed utterly ridiculous to Martin. Moving on through the activities suggested, he veered away from everything with 'adrenaline-fuelled' in the strapline and wondered once again what it was he was actually going to do in New Zealand. He was really looking forward to seeing Gerry of course, and catching up, but now doubt assailed him. Could you just 'catch up' for five weeks? Martin briefly ran through their shared years, and the space in between, which now seemed rather paltry and perhaps not worth looking back upon. Gerry had spoken, by email, of the building of the garden room, in which Martin was to stay, and mentioned that he had plans for an upgrade for his garage. He wondered if the upgrade might be imminent - perhaps they could work together, but then again, a garage upgrade would be a very personal project. Martin allowed himself to imagine upgrading his own garage - for which there was no need, as it was exactly how he wanted it in every way - but could not picture himself wanting or allowing anybody to help him with such a thing. The placing of plug sockets for example was a one-man job based on very personal and firmly held ideals, beliefs and needs. Over the years, Martin had developed a range of outwardly awkward fixes to problems which would traditionally require a second pair of hands. It made him utterly self-reliant, if somewhat prone to freak accidents and using more materials than originally intended. So, no, he did not really believe that he and Gerry would work harmoniously on Gerry's garage upgrade.

He sighed, closed down the computer and went to make himself a hot drink before bed. While the kettle boiled, he consoled himself with the thought that it was only five weeks, and he firmly believed that as long as you had an end date in mind you could endure anything.

Chapter 21

Martin took his seat gratefully on the plane. Getting to and through the airport had been seamless, thanks to extensive planning and a dry run on the airport rail link some weeks ago, but it had still been tiring. He had stowed his hand luggage and dripping waterproof jacket in the locker above his head and once he had fastened his seat belt he was able to look around him. A window seat was always interesting, even in this rain, but he had agonised over perhaps booking an aisle seat. He was, thus far, happy with his choice, looking out over the airport and seeing the baggage handlers going about their business. So engrossed was he with their shoddy treatment of people's personal possessions that he had no time to quail at the sight of a mother and smallish child making a beeline towards the two empty seats to his left.

She hefted herself and the squirming child into the seats, startling Martin as she caught him on the shoulder with a bag seemingly filled with breeze blocks. Martin politely hid his pain, but his heart sank nonetheless. Six hours and fifty-five minutes to Dubai. The woman apologised lightly, but not before the child reached out and grabbed for his glasses, smearing the lenses with something partially digested. Martin remained polite but decided that as soon as they were airborne, he would feign sleep as purposefully as possible.

An hour and a half in, and Martin was still playing peepo with the inflight magazine. The child, who Martin reluctantly knew was called Chelsey, spelt C-HAITCH-E-L-S-E-Y, shrieked in delight every time Martin disappeared behind the pages of duty free offers and perfume adverts, then forcefully ripped yet another page away with her chubby hand, to reveal his increasingly thin smile.

Chelsey's mother was well into her third in-flight gin, and Martin felt that she could no longer be reasonably or safely relied upon for help, but he was running out of entertainment options. He had just held up the magazine again when the announcement came for passengers to put on their seat belts. Turbulence, apparently. Martin smugly noted his own secure seatbelt, never released since he'd put it on, long before takeoff, but felt it his duty to help Chelsey and her mother, who was more than a little fumbly with her fingers.

The turbulence continued and a sudden burst of thunder brought murmurs and shifting from his fellow passengers. Lightening followed and suddenly the plane jolted alarmingly and began to list and tilt, clearly now on a downward trajectory. Lights flashed off and on, then came back on dimly, assisted by the emergency lighting strips that ran along the aisle. Loud rushing noises filled the whole plane, air spiralling and streaming around, blowing the inflight magazine finally to pieces. The pages whirled in the air, fascinating and horrifying Martin in equal measure. A sudden powerful blast of icy air pinned Martin to his seat, the extreme cold forcing the hairs on his arms to instant attention. He squirmed back against the seat, his bare legs scraping against the harsh itchy weave of the seat covering. The sensations were intense, dressed as he was in only his vest and underpants. Nobody else seemed to share Martin's sense of urgency and panic; Chelsey's mother offered him carrot sticks from a Tupperware tub whilst balancing her plastic gin glass on the seat arm. Chelsey herself was nowhere to be seen, but Martin was pinned to his seat, unable to move. The plane was really gathering speed now and it was inevitable that a crash must soon take place, but the fall went on and on. Water had started to pool around Martin's feet, rising above his socks, the cheerful plane and cloud motif chosen with such care that morning now seemed so utterly out of place. As the water began to lap towards his knees, Martin braced for impact - it must come soon. He had been one of the few passengers to really pay attention during the air steward's presentation. He tucked his head and arms in front of him, shouting "Brace, brace, brace," but the words wouldn't come out...

Tangled, hot and breathless, he woke up. In his own bed, curtains blowing out through the open window, gentle rain falling outside his own home. Which he was choosing to leave in less than three hours' time. Practical as ever, Martin reached out and put on his bedside light, got up and closed the window, redrawing the curtains against the morning darkness with a confidence he didn't feel. He drank his bedside water standing up, beside his bed. He waited until his heart was beating normally again, but he couldn't return to bed. Not because it was too crumpled, sweaty and disturbed, but because the other side, Sheila's side, was as smooth and pristine it had been for the last ten years. It was time to get up and get on.

Chapter 22

Alan's first solo day at the shop went unbelievably well. Absolutely nothing bad happened. No disasters, no emergency evacuation procedures, no unexpected deliveries.

The lady from the suppliers they used most frequently phoned just after 10.30, and was obviously not surprised not to speak to Martin. She had been informed by email as a priority some weeks ago, so it was really just a courtesy call to see how Alan was getting on. He was able to report that the first hour and half of being in sole charge had been uneventful. She seemed pleased to hear this, but Alan picked up a hesitancy in her delivery, possibly an uncertainty that he was up to the job? Or was he reading too much into this?

He filled the space by telling her about some of the intricacies of the filing system, keen to show her that he was competent without giving away too much. She seemed only mildly interested and he tailed off, expecting her to wind up the call. She didn't.

"So, Alan," she began, "as you know, we've been supplying Martin for many years..."

This was not news to Alan, but he was conditioned to agree politely with a lady.

"And, obviously, he has a great deal of understanding of his customer base, and he is a good customer with ourselves too. As you will no doubt be aware, we are preparing his usual monthly order currently, with a view to delivery next week."

Again, Alan agreed, but he couldn't help but hear something in her tone which alarmed him. Something was coming.

"As a regular and valued customer, we are very familiar with Martin's requirements, and of course, I can reassure you that those requirements will be met by ourselves. The reason for my call, Alan, if I may..." She paused, neither of them knowing why, but equally fascinated as to what the outcome would be.

Alan experienced a brief misting of his glasses, a mere passing thing, perhaps nothing.

"Is to offer you an opportunity, at no charge to yourself "(she knew her mark) "to stock, on a trial basis, a new range that we have developed, with the younger modeller in mind?"

Alan felt his silence expand, thicken and then solidify. She went on, encouraged.

"So, do you have a minute now, Alan, so I can talk you through the opportunity?"

Alan's eyes darted over the empty shop, the sleeping dog, the weak wintery sunshine cutting low over the boxes and boxes of unsold tanks, submarines and bi-planes.

He felt the undead spirit of Martin looming behind him on the plinth, his slight other-worldly presence creaking the boards of the plinth, his absent sightless eyes peering piercingly over his shoulder. This was so not part of the plan.

A little prickle of electricity shot through him, blood left his rational brain and returned at full throttle to the mad impetuous part of his brain that had last seen action in the butcher's shop with Nathan.

"Certainly, yes, go on..."

*

By the time Nathan and Troy came pinging through the door just after 3.30, Alan was absolutely fit to burst with the news. The boys were beyond impressed. They had both been aware of this new range (Model Club could talk of nothing else), focussing as it did on the worlds of sci-fi, anime and manga, but never in their wildest dreams did they imagine that Alan would be the unassuming vehicle that brought it within their grasp. Their amazement knew no bounds when Alan explained that the suppliers had asked him not only to stock the kits, but were also going to supply, for free, two kits that the boys could build and display in the shop, the better to engage and interest the younger modeller.

The kits were due in the following Tuesday, and so preparations had to be made. They agreed that, if Ernest could be moved, they could set up a work table in the shop window, where the models could be built, in situ, by the boys after school. Posters and publicity materials would be provided, and Alan had prepared a small piece for the local paper. Troy and Nathan exchanged meaningful glances when Alan announced this and carefully read them his draft piece, but it was up to Nathan, as a blood relative, to explain why this was totally lame.

"Yeah, that's really good Grandad."

Troy looked at the floor.

"The thing is, Mr, er, Alan, don't you think it would be good if, maybe, you put it on the socials?"

Alan smiled pleasantly. "I think it will just go in the news section."

Troy tried again. "The thing is, me and Nathan, we could maybe get it on Facebook? Put it on Insta? Share it with our mates?"

Alan smiled pleasantly.

"Of course. Please do tell your friends. We need lots of youngsters."

"Ok, so, that's okay with you Grandad, if we make an account, tag in the suppliers?"

Alan seemed alarmed at the use of the word account. This implied something financial to him. The beauty of this whole exercise was that it wasn't going to cost any of them any money at all.

Troy and Nathan were able to explain what sort of account they meant, and talk Alan through his fuddled, bewildered questions to the point where he caved in and gave permission. He wasn't entirely sure what it all meant, but it was legal and free and maybe, today, after the mighty leap he had made, that was enough for him.

Chapter 23

The promised kits, and the rest of November's order duly arrived on Tuesday, leaving Alan the rest of the week to prepare for Saturday, the big launch day. He had been rather taken aback at the amount of publicity material the company had sent, and was now in a quandary about how to fix the many posters to the walls. Obviously sellotape was a no-no, as any homeowner or person responsible for their own paintwork knows, but he really didn't know how he felt about Blu Tack. Of course, it would certainly mark the paintwork if left on for a significant period of time, but he envisaged these posters being up for a maximum of 10 days and despite extensive research, he could not find a definitive number of days that would leave the walls blemish free. He then researched various brands, focussing initially on White Tack, which he quickly realised only differed from Blu Tack by being white and made by a different company. This led him down a fascinating rabbit hole on the development of numerous products, but by 12.30 he had come to the conclusion that it was simply too risky to use any kind of sticky substance on walls that were not his own. How could he begin to cover over the potential damage without redecorating entirely? It wasn't that he wouldn't be able to match the paint, as Martin had shown him the folder for the maintenance schedule, and pointed out the make, shade and finish of each type of paint used on every surface. The bigger difficulty was that the main shop interior walls were not due to be repainted for another two and a half years, (although the exterior paintwork was due in January, he noted) and there was sure to be a discrepancy between any new patches and old paintwork.

Luckily, no customers interrupted Alan's research and so, by 2 o'clock, he had been able to sketch out the perfect solution. He had plenty of suitable off-cuts at home, and was quite excited about getting started on three easel-style arrangements and one long hanging bar that could be fixed above the interior of the shop window and allow the posters to hang freely. He was unsure about how he would weight the bottoms of the posters to prevent unwanted edge curl, but he had in mind some balsa wood batons that might do the trick.

As well as the posters, there was a large cardboard upright stand, about his height when he had finished slotting flap A into flap L and then affixing both firmly to point T. It was quite imposing, and he stood back to take in the full effect, still untroubled as he was by customers. The black and brown tones of the creature's armour were picked out with jewel-red details, which nicely echoed the blood dripping from its sword. It wore a partial helmet, the side portions of which framed its...not-face. A series of symmetrical lumps and tubular connections wove together around a possible mouth, and where one would expect eyes to be, two fiercely glowing holes were implied. Martin felt that the quality of the printing was excellent, but as he didn't know what it was meant to be, he couldn't say if it was a reasonable likeness or not. It compared well with the pictures on the boxes of the new kits though, and Alan presumed that the boys would be pleased.

The boys. Alan smiled quietly to himself. The boys. Without him noticing, care of Nathan had moved from a duty to a joy. He still made an awful lot of mince-based meals, but thanks to Nathan, he could at least now buy it repacked at a reasonable price from the supermarket. He had recently begun introducing pork tenderloin into his repertoire, as it had been on special offer, and it had been a great success, with everyone praising his (homemade) barbecue sauce. He had been inspired to go further, and tonight's meal, to which Troy had been invited, was to be a pork stir fry. Alan had bought two packs of pre-prepared stir-fry vegetables. He had carefully calculated the economy of doing so, having done a thorough inventory and price comparison of buying the individual vegetables, to say nothing of his time costs in preparing them. Also, he really wasn't sure where he would buy small quantities of bean sprouts and had baulked at the idea of visiting the out-of-town oriental supermarket beyond the ring road.

The pork had been marinating since the previous day and he knew that cooking rice was well within his capabilities, so he was tentatively looking forward to preparing the meal. The only cloud on his culinary horizon was a worry that he should have bought prawn crackers. He remembered Jackie doing them a couple of times, little beige biscuits that had to be held down in the deep fat fryer, transforming miraculously into light white ovals of mildly fishy polystyrene. He still had the deep fat fryer - it was in a box in the garage - but the idea of using it did not appeal. Jackie had known what she was doing with it, but it made him anxious just thinking about the potential for danger. Many times had he read of house fires caused by deep fat fryers ('Mum of three praises plucky firefighters', 'Lucky escape for Lucy the Labrador' and 'Tragic end for wartime hero'...) although he knew that the root cause of the fire was not the chip pan itself, but negligence and a casual attitude to safety, neither of which would be a factor in his own life. Still, he thought generally he would rather not use the thing, and resolved to pick up a ready-done packet on his way home.

The afternoon moved slowly on, with one customer who was somewhere between interested and horrified at the display going up. The poor man had only come in to pick up some glue he had ordered. He had very specific adhesive needs, which Alan respected of course, but there had been some difficulty about the price. The gentleman had ordered it in person from Martin some weeks ago, and was expecting the price he had been quoted. Unfortunately, it fell under the new stock prices and there was a discrepancy of some 45p. Alan had to think on his feet and made a snap decision to honour the original price, but once the man had gone, his hand went to the small change he always carried in his pocket. Sticking to your principles - in this case, non-confrontation - could be expensive he mused, as he sorted the coins into the till.

He was just turning to put the kettle on, thinking to steady his nerves with a nice cup of tea, when Nathan and Troy came pinging in. They brought with them the tang of cold winter air and Nathan's normally pale face was transformed into the healthy look of a 1930's farm boy, as if fresh from apple scrumping and pre-manly exertions. The boys were clearly animated and continued talking and jostling each other as they came into the shop. Ernest responded in kind and leapt to his feet, circling and wagging from boy to boy. He always had to be reminded not to jump up because of his back, and mostly the boys just hurled themselves on the floor to avoid the issue, but today, for once, something more important than Ernest stopped them in their tracks.

Chapter 24

"Woah!" cried out Troy, spinning to fully face the enormous cardboard cut-out that stood imposingly on the shop floor.

"Oh my days! Avalar! That is sooo cool!" chimed in Nathan.

"Avalar, is like, the most evil of all the villains, this is going to be so awesome Mr, er, Alan. Did the kits arrive too?"

Alan merely smiled and used his hand to direct the boys' attention to the table set up in the spot previously taken up by Ernest's basket. He found that he was enjoyed being the facilitator to so much joy.

The boys rushed over to the table, subconsciously negotiating Ernest's ignored windings under their feet. They pressed themselves against the table, knuckles white against the edge, just enjoying looking at the two large boxes before them. Lurid manga-style depictions of creatures dripping with slime and blood covered the fronts of the boxes, and although all the instructions and writing were in English, it had been given a Japanese-style font.

Alan came over to join them, hands dug proprietorially into his trouser pockets.

"So, these are the two kits they have sent. Do they meet with your approval?" he asked, knowing what the answer would be.

The boys and Alan spent the next half hour examining the exterior of the kits and planning how best to carry out the build, deciding eventually that the boys would have one of the kits already made, for display purposes, but that the other could be used as a sort of 'stunt kit' and be made 'live' in the shop on Saturday as part of the launch. Once they had decided which kit best fitted which role, they had only to collect their personal choice of glue. It did, of course, come with glue, but as Martin had always said (regularly, ad infinitum): "A modeller is only ever as good as his glue." This truism had been pressed home on the boys since the first time they had, separately, met Martin, and they now felt it was worth repeating, in unison, when Alan began to say it. He acknowledged the humour in their joining in and grandly said that he would personally pay for the glue himself, so everybody felt pretty good by closing time.

Alan did his pre-departure checks, the boys collected Ernest's possessions and of course the kit and the glue, and they all walked together back towards the pork stir fry.

Alan initially felt a little excluded as he rustled around opening bags of vegetables and removing cling film in the kitchen, but he caught himself in time, hearing Jackie's voice reminding him to let them be as they set up for the make on the table in the sitting room. He wasn't sure where they would eat this stir fry, but he knew that their enthusiasm should not be squashed by him shooing them off and putting down place mats and a soy sauce bottle. Ernest was right under his feet during the cooking process, but it was actually quite nice to have his company. He looked down at the ever-hopeful little dog, wagging up at him, his eyes willing him to drop the whole bowl of marinated pork loin.

"No, Ernest, this is people food. Not for you, my boy." There was warmth and compassion in his voice and Ernest got that, but it was useless to him. All he wanted was food. If he had known the phrase, "Fine words don't butter no parsnips," he would have used it. Sadly, he did not, so he did the next best thing; he wagged a little harder. Ernest knew how to push a lot of human buttons, but he had not quite worked out all of Alan's. However, he was nothing if not persistent and continued his intense observation of Alan's culinary progress.

Every now and then, Alan would leave his catering and silently pad through to look at the boys, hunched over the table and completely engrossed in their task. He had not known that modelling could be anything other than a solo occupation until his relationship with Nathan changed. The Day of the Mince, that was when he thought it began, and what a good day that had been. Obviously not the part where he had been mistaken for a paedophile, or actually the bit where Nathan had told him and the butcher to fuck off, well, more him he supposed. "Buy your own fucking mince," were his actual words, but the message was clear enough. However the fact that they'd been forced to talk about it, that it had led to Nathan making those first two models, and that he could now buy cheaper mince elsewhere were all huge breakthroughs as far as Alan was concerned.

By the time Claire arrived, the boys were well on the way with the build, deeply engaged with minute detail and huge concentration. She had her own key but sometimes it was just easier to ring the doorbell, especially after the day she had had. Alan bustled to let her in, wiping his hands on a tea towel as he went. He took one look at her stricken face and with only a heartbeat's pause said,

"A505?"

Claire nodded silently, walking past him whilst removing her scarf and coat. The evenings were colder now, darker too, and it only took one whiff of roadworks to foul up a person's whole journey home. She hung up her jacket by its furry hood and laid her scarf on top so that the ends hung symmetrically.

"It just doesn't get any better Dad. Yesterday, I had to be in Peterborough by 8.30. An hour and twenty should have been plenty at that time of day, but I didn't get there until just gone quarter to."

Alan tried not to look shocked, but Claire knew him too well.

"What? An hour and a half, tops! I left at 7.10, on the dot." She leant her back against the work surface, spreading her hands out to her sides, fingers splayed across the beige formica. She fixed her gaze on her left hand, hoping to convey interest in the state of her nail polish.

Alan pursed his lips, deciding not to challenge her and busied himself with weighing out the rice. The dial rose painfully slowly as he poured the rice into the white rectangular plastic container which fitted neatly onto the ageing red plastic body of the scales. As he neared 200 grammes, he slowed even more, but once he had reached his goal, he put the rice bag down more firmly than he meant to. He turned to face Claire.

"The journey itself is of course, possible in an hour and twenty minutes, but you have to take into account the temporary speed restrictions on the A1 and you know as well as I do, it only takes some idiot to get in the wrong lane when you come off at those lights by Homebase and the whole system collapses."

Claire turned shiftily to examine the nail polish on her right hand. She knew he was right.

Chapter 25

Saturday involved an early start, so everybody involved would need to be prepped and ready the night before. After closing, Alan, Nathan, Troy, Ernest and Claire had gathered at the shop. It was Claire's first visit and her being there gave everybody a mingled sense of pride and awkwardness. Ernest felt the heightened sense of occasion and disgraced himself against the Humbrol paint display rack. Nathan and Troy saw him do it, but a quick glance between them confirmed that they would neither be dobbing him in nor rushing to clean it up. Claire was the 'first' to notice it, swerving dramatically to avoid the puddle on her way past with a pile of magazines that Alan had asked her to bring in from the car. She plonked the box down on the plinth and returned stoically to the kitchenette where she presumed, correctly, she would find kitchen paper and Flash.

Having cleaned up, she returned to her original task. She could see that her father had prepared a cloth-covered table at the back of the shop, with a small folded laminated sign, suggesting people help themselves to a magazine in return for a donation. Alan hadn't discussed it with anybody, and Claire knew better than to make a thing of him getting rid of long held possessions, but she allowed herself a small private smile as she saw what he had organised and began to quietly think of likely recipients for the charity donations. Retired Modellers Benevolent Fund? Pernicketty Pedants Support Group? She remembered her mother had always gently teased Alan about his inability to throw anything away, his storing, cataloging and keeping 'just in case.' She was always careful not to tease him too much though, and Claire remembered how she had never made a big deal of his collecting, ending every discussion with the same phrase, "Lucky for you, I like squirrels."

Reaching out to pick up the tin, she took a sharp intake of breath as she made sense of the logo she saw carefully printed and laminated on the side and lid. A cartoon squirrel wearing a sling and the words 'Red Squirrel Rehabilitation Centre, Keswick.' Her mother had indeed, always liked squirrels... Claire replaced the tin and took a few moments to compose herself.

*

Within an hour or so, everything was ready. Ernest had been lashed to the table leg to prevent more bad behaviour and had so far done very little to make the evening all about him. The posters and their hanging arrangements looked fabulous, everyone agreed. Claire said it took her right back to her teenage bedroom and started to explain about posters of bands she'd liked that none of the males present knew anything about, although Alan was touched that his hanging arrangements then had been appreciated and remembered after all this time. They politely waited for her to finish reminiscing, then carried on with their appraisal of the set up. The boys were happy with the display of their finished model of Avalar in his lair, complete with garage parking. It would be the first thing people would see, placed as it was right in the centre of the plinth.

The live modelling display was set up to everyone's satisfaction, although looking at the table in front of the window made Nathan's stomach lurch. He suddenly realised how very public it would be. Yes, he had a friend in Troy, he now had a good relationship with his Grandad and his very own dog, but you didn't have to scratch very deep to find the Nathan who had chosen to lurk under the radar for the vast majority of his life. For the first time in a long time, he shrugged on his coat and flipped up the hood, then looked firmly at the floor.

"Ready to go Nathan?' asked Claire.

"Yup," he said, untying Ernest from the table leg.

Troy was unaffected, and carried on twittering on about who was coming from Model Club (Tyler, Sam, Charlie, Jahaan and possibly Ethan) and what his dad's friend Andy had said about the upcoming Nationals in Telford (classes were going to be larger, more entries would be from Eastern Europe) whilst getting under Alan's feet during the lock up process.

Alan shooed them all out of the shop and gave himself a moment in the empty but visually busy shop. He took a deep breath, in and then out. He looked over to the little squirrel on the logo. Yes, it would be okay.

Chapter 26

They had all agreed to be at the shop by 9 am, ready for a 10 am opening, but Alan had woken early and felt that once he had got dressed and had breakfast, there was no point in him being at home any longer.

As he turned around the corner off the High Street, his brain could not make sense of the sheer number of people lined up on the pavement outside the shop. He drove more and more slowly to try and see what was going on. At least twenty figures, most of them with hoods up and phones held before them were neatly lined up along the shopfront. Peering out, he leant forward in the car, his neck stretched out to give him a better view over the steering wheel. As he studied the figures, he saw that they were almost all young, maybe Nathan's age, although some were taller and clearly more mature. Some even had facial hair, but one little lad was with his mum, holding her hand and bouncing on the spot. He felt a horrible lurch of recognition as soon as he locked eyes with the boy's mother. Last seen in her rear-view mirror, fixed intently on his pathetic attempt to act normal around his grandson, her expression was the same as it had been on the day of the mince. Of course, she recognised him instantly, it was clear from the way she pulled her son in tight that she was still deeply suspicious of his motives, and now, here he was, driving slowly past a group of largely pre-pubescent boys. Her gave her what he hoped was a reassuring wave and indicated into the parking space at the side of the shop. The locking bollard was a godsend parking-wise, but it could be temperamental and Alan fumbled the keys in his agitated state. What were these people doing here? And what time had they arrived, for goodness sake? It was still only 7.05 and even in the time it had taken him to kerb crawl to a halt, another three youths had joined the throng.

His arrival caused a flutter of interest in the queue, and Alan had to ask the lead lad to step back a little so he could get to the door. He had by now realised that they must all be here for the launch, but was compelled to say, "Are you here for the launch?" to which the lead lad nodded several times and said, "Yeah, yeah, I am."

Alan wasn't sure where to go with this, but rallied with, "Yes, well, good. Excellent," then let himself into the shop without further comment.

He made straight for the kitchenette, filling a mug with cold water and pouring it unsteadily into the empty kettle. Whilst the water boiled he made himself focus on the beauty of regular descaling. He found that during moments of uncertainty it helped to dwell on that which he found reassuring and soothing, in this case, energy efficiency, lack of limescale and improved appliance lifespan. By the time he had made his coffee he was calm enough to be able to do a surreptitious headcount, reckoning that there must be at least 30 people outside the shop now. The lady from the Day of the Mince was watching his every move, which he found unnerving but understandable, but everyone else was just staring into their phones, prepared for a long wait.

Just before 9 o'clock, Nathan and Claire banged on the door, wanting to be let in. He had been sitting reading one of the magazines he had brought in, with his back to the window, and their arrival startled him. He let them in immediately, explaining clearly for the benefit of the queue that they were staff and that he was glad to see them, which he really was. Nathan was full of it, talking over Alan's careful re-locking of the shop door.

"Grandad! The queue goes all the way down to the bus stop! There's like, maybe, 200 people!"

Claire inclined her head slightly, and looked at her father.

"Well, maybe not that many, Nathan, but certainly, a lot. And yes, right down to the bus stop. I had no idea, did you Dad?"

Alan did not. He had never seen anything like this before. And he remembered when Airfix brought out The Showjumper, a kit that was part of a series they hoped would encourage girls to make models too. Airfix hotly denied it was Princess Anne, but it certainly looked like her, and she had just won a silver medal in the 1975 European Eventing Championships, so a considerable buzz accompanied the launch of that particular model, but nothing like this.

Just then, Troy splatted against the glass in the manner of a pigeon hitting a window. His flattened cheek and ear mangled against his coat and beanie hat as the leading lad in the queue pinned him aggressively to the shop window. Alan rapped sharply on the glass and wagged his finger, whilst Claire unlocked the door and faced up to the lad.

"Staff!" she belted, her face right up against the leading lad's. She pulled a protective arm around Troy's shocked form and dragged him in.

"Alright?" Troy nodded, his face aglow with excitement and abrasion.

"Did you see them? The queue goes past the bus stop, round on to the High Street, all the way to the travel agents. I can't believe it!"

Alan took off his glasses to polish them.

"I can't believe this many people read *The Comet*. Last time I heard, sales were right down and nobody bothered with local papers. I'll be thanking Alastair for putting my piece in about the launch, I can tell you."

Nathan and Troy exchanged glances just as Alan looked up.

"And of course, you boys told your friends, no doubt," he added, not wanting them to feel that their juvenile efforts had been insignificant.

"Yeah, yeah, we did," nodded Troy, "but it got picked up by @tommakes on Instagram?" He lifted the end of his sentence, expecting at least a flutter of something from Alan and Claire. Nathan was speechless, eyes wide and hands dangling down and splayed in shock. Troy tried again.

"@tommakes? No? Really? He's like, he's, help me out Nathan! He's incredible! He's got like, a hundred thousand likes! Have you really not heard of him Mr er Alan. He reviews and makes kits, documents the process, posts really cool pictures, amazing dioramas. I mean, the way he makes water look... he once did this jet, taking off, with, like, actual smoke made of some kind of fibre, it was awesome!"

Everyone still looked a bit stunned.

"Well, anyway," Troy took it down a notch or two, "he's posted about our launch, and it's already got like, 50,000 likes." He waited expectantly.

"Sorry, 50,000 like whats? I'm not following."

"It means it's really popular and lots of people know about the launch, Dad," explained Claire.

"But, 50,000," mused Alan, looking anxiously at the small A5 sheet he had prepared to note down orders he could not fulfil from the 30 kits currently in stock. "We're going to need a bigger order book.'

"Ha, nice one, Alan!" Troy put on his best American accent, "We're gonna need a bigger order book!" He looked around at his challenged audience, but nobody reacted, so he said it again, finishing with a quick rendition of the theme from *Jaws*. Nothing. These people.

Alan led them all back to the kitchenette, away from the glare of mince-day lady, wondering if he did indeed have a bigger order book.

Between themselves they agreed that Nathan and Troy would build the second kit as planned, and Alan would remain plinth-bound, man the till and generally supervise. Claire's role had not been pre-considered, but based on her performance in dealing with leading lad, it was now clear that she would be in charge of security. There was bound to be jostling, she had a hi-vis tabard in her handbag, and after the week she'd had driving up and down the A1, she had a lot of inner rage that could usefully be redirected. Claire quickly saw that they would need a one-way system to mange the flow of youths and persuaded her father that with minimal disruption, customers could be routed in past the plinth, round the stunt modelling set up, back around the Woodland Scenics carousel to the plinth, then with the addition of a carefully placed cone, back out past the kitchenette and into the rear car parking area. Alan wasn't sure this would work and was concerned that so many people seeing these 'back rooms' could compromise security and even potentially invalidate the insurance in the event of a subsequent break in, but Claire had the bit between her teeth, and actually, it was a triumph of crowd control.

They had settled on allowing only eight customers in the shop at any one time and Nathan and Troy had knocked up a very good sign making this clear, using the same font as that on the boxed kits. They had synchronised their watches and the shop clock, and Claire was ready at the door. As the clock twitched finally to 10 o'clock, Alan turned to Claire, nodded, and the day began.

Chapter 27

Claire leant heavily against the back door as she felt it give and then click shut, enjoying the ensuing silence. Silence. For the first time since 10 o'clock this morning, the shop was quiet. Alan exhaled deeply and leant firmly on the plinth. They could still hear the last of the customers outside in the parking area, gathering under the orange glow of the street lamp for selfies and grinning thumbs-up photos of themselves with their bags, but nobody in the shop moved. Troy had theatrically thrown his head down on to the table and allowed his arms to dangle lifelessly at his sides. Nathan was sitting bolt upright next to him, staring into the middle distance, oblivious to the spitter of rain on the shop window, the swish of tyres on the wet road and the muted chatter of the last of Saturday's shoppers heading home in the almost dark.

Claire broke first, pulling herself up to her full height, stretching her head and shoulders back. A few tendrils of hair had escaped from her tight ponytail and caught loosely on the open weave of her hi-vis. She felt her neck crick, and did a few more experimental stretches.

"476," she announced.

"476? Are you sure?" queried Alan. "It felt like a lot more than that."

"Completely accurate, Dad," smiled Claire, holding up the chrome tally counter she wore on her work lanyard. "476, and I know that's accurate because I counted each and every one of them out of this door."

"What about that blonde girl that came back with her other friend again later?" smirked Troy, looking meaningfully at Nathan. "Did you count her twice? The one that fancied Nathan?" He made big eyes and a kissy face right in Nathan's personal space.

"She did not," blushed Nathan furiously, shoulder barging Troy.

"She did too," shoulder barged Troy back.

"Thank you, boys," Claire interrupted smoothly, "I recognised her, actually, when she came back, so I didn't count her twice." Claire recognised her because she too had noticed the girl's obvious interest in Nathan, and it made her smile and actually feel a little emotional at the time. She had been fighting off girls on Matt's behalf for some years now, answering the door to their breathless enquiries about Matt's whereabouts and kindly explaining that she would be sure to give him the message to call, but now it was happening for Nathan too.

"She's called Chloe," grinned Troy helpfully. "She's in my English set. Chloe and Nathan, sitting in a tree, K, I..."

He didn't get a chance to finish though, as Nathan swooped up his anorak off the back of the chair and extinguished Troy entirely from sight and sound, holding the coat firmly around his neck with the crook of his arm.

"Steady on boys, steady on. Looks like you two need to let off steam. Claire and I will tidy up here, you two get off home and take Ernest out for a run. He'll be absolutely busting, shut up since lunchtime."

The boys laughed and jostled their way out of the shop, their departure leaving a different silence between Claire and Alan. A communal, satisfied silence, like an empty box of shared Maltesers.

"What a day. What. A. Day. Shall we have a cup of tea before we do anything else, Dad?"

"Absolutely. I'll get the kettle on. Sit down, Claire, you must be done in."

"D'you know, I'm not? I mean, yes, I'm tired, but, I mean, that was absolutely bloody brilliant! The enthusiasm! Those kids, so full of it all. Nathan and Troy - weren't they amazing? So confident and good with all the questions. And the sheer volume of sales - the shop's practically stripped clean!"

Over the noise of the kettle boiling Alan called back, "Quite honestly Claire, if we hadn't had you, it would have been a disaster. I don't know how you did it. That woman with the rucksack? I'd have killed her, but the way you handled it... And when we had to tell them we'd run out of kits? You turned it around, made everyone feel like a VIP, got them signing up in the BIGGER order book, ha! The one-way system was a triumph, and the way you got those kids eating out of your hand... you just took everything in your stride, quite a skill Claire."

*

Claire looked down at the tally counter, last used in her role as Fire Warden at work. She closed her eyes. She felt herself glowing internally, adrenaline from the day still buzzing around her body, but this honest admiration from her father was the cherry on the top. She had loved every minute of the day, directing operations, breaking up fights, de-escalating difficult glue-based situations and generally making things run like clockwork. She had been nervous at first, not that anybody would have known. She had stood tall, exuding outward authority and calm, even if inside, her heart had been thumping. People listened when she asked them to step aside, people asked her where the toilet was, people nodded seriously and understandingly when she explained about the shortage of kits. They believed her when she said that they would receive a phone call as soon as the kits arrived and it was her that they gave a cheery last wave to.

"Here's your tea, Claire."

"Thanks Dad."

"Well, thank you."

They both looked towards the empty magazine box at the squirrel logo.

"She'd be proud of you, CC. She really would."

"You too, Dad, you too."

Chapter 28

C. That took her back. Claire Carol Barnwell was how she started life. She had always enjoyed her mother telling her the story of her name as a little girl, and she smiled at the memory of it now. Apparently, during the pregnancy, her parents had gone back and forth discussing the name of their unborn baby, and right from the start Jackie had had a strong feeling that she was carrying another little boy. The due date was 17th December, and so she had wanted to mark the nearness to Christmas with the name Noel. Alan had not been particularly keen on the name, bringing to mind the presenter Noel Edmunds who he'd seen on *Top Gear* a couple of times, but it was well before the Mr Blobby years and Jackie hadn't even heard of him, so that counted for nothing. Alan had acquiesced to Jackie's choice and they had agreed that in the unlikely event of it being a girl, he could pick the name. He had chosen Claire, with an i, having had an Auntie Claire (a neighbour, no relation) who he had loved as a child and since lost touch with. He checked the name in the Book of Baby Names that Jackie had borrowed from the library and was pleased to see that it meant 'bright' or 'clear', both of which he hoped their child would be.

The 17th December came and went, and of course, Claire had finally been born on the 25th, Christmas Day at 6.05am. Jackie was astonished to be told it was a little girl and corrected the medical staff, surely they meant boy? But no, it was a little girl and she wept tears of joy and relief. That was what she had really wanted, she told Claire, but to save herself from disappointment, she had firmly imagined and believed she was having a boy. The arrival of a girl, not the expected boy, meant that Noel was no longer an option, so Claire it was. However, Jackie still hankered after a seasonal reference, and pushed for Carol, but Alan made her see sense, fearing teasing and unhappiness for this tiny new person's future as Christmas Carol.

They compromised on Carol as a middle name, so, CC became the family pet name, used predominantly by her father. He had gradually stopped using it at her teenage request and the more mature sounding Claire suited her better anyway.

CC. She smiled again, remembering her childhood alter ego, PC CC. She had developed a fascination for the police from her earliest days of watching *Postman Pat* and being obsessed with PC Selby. She received a tiny police dressing up outfit for her second birthday and was rarely seen out of it and its larger replacements before she was forced into school uniform at five. Robert had first coined the name PC CC and they would say it repeatedly to a special tune which made them laugh like drains until they could barely breathe, and once, memorably, laughed so much that Claire was a little bit sick in her mouth, which had made Robert at least laugh even harder.

There was a photo, she visualised it now, of the two of them sitting at the bottom of the stairs, Claire looming over Robert in a tiny hi-vis and hat, hands on hips, him dressed as a laughing burglar in a stripy jumper and black eye mask. They must have been about three and five respectively she thought, long before he became the isolated, distant black-clad young man who hid his face under a curtain of dark hair. The two images of Robert were at odds, and Claire struggled to think which one was the one she really remembered. She had been moving away from the world of the family before he died, developing her own identity, looking to friends for advice and support, and so his dark door-slamming and silent forced participation at family events had not really concerned her.

Obviously, his death had been horrific, a time of extreme desolation and blank survival, but she was her own person, with her own life to lead, and her friends and school work had been her primary focus away from the overwhelming shock and sadness that characterised her home life. That focus on schoolwork and achieving good grades had unwittingly taken her away from her childhood dream to join the police. The better her grades, the more her teachers seduced her with the promise of university first, then the police, if she still wanted it. BSc in hand, life got in the way, she married Carl, had Matt and then Nathan, and now...

Claire was sufficiently motivated by these reminiscences to get up from the sofa, away from the inane blue glare of the late-night television and search out the photo. She knew exactly where it would be; red album, top shelf, about half way along. There was a point where the albums stopped, the digital age having overtaken her love of curating physical photos, but this was an actual picture, circa 1983 or 4, and she, like Google but slower and wearing a floppy cardigan, was able to locate it with ease.

Holding the album open on her knees, Claire tried angling the page so she could see the photo without the glare and disruption of the brittle cellophane that had protected it all these years. Irritated, she peeled back the transparent layer to reveal the naked photo. She had forgotten the special texture of photographs from her youth. Smooth, yet pockmarked, splitting the light like the surface of an orange. Carefully she peeled the picture off the once-adhesive backing and held it close to her face. There they were - Robert, not at all how he was, and her, not at all how she was. A police officer was all she had ever wanted to be until her head was turned by academic success. Not that having good grades would have precluded her from joining the force, it was just somehow the grades, and promise of more academic success shone more brightly than her original ambition.

What had her father said today? "You just took it all in your stride." Well, she had. And loved every minute of it. And came home buzzing. And thinking. About PC CC, and how she'd never had the chance to be. At uni, she'd briefly thought about it, but then she'd met Carl and he was in pharmaceuticals and it all seemed so glamorous. Ha. She could never have done the shift work anyhow, when Matt and Nathan were younger, what with Carl's hectic man-child skater-boy lifestyle filling every weekend as it was, but now? Would it be possible? She picked up her phone and typed in "maximum age to join the police UK."

Just.

Time was ticking, but she was fit, she was keen and there was never going to be a better time for PC CC to come out of the closet.

Chapter 29

Monday morning in the shop could have felt very flat after the excitement of Saturday, but in fact, the phone rang constantly; not only people placing orders but also suppliers who had got wind of the launch and now wanted to be part of it in some way. Alan had to delve deep into his reserves of pleasantness to respond appropriately as the morning went on. He had been looking forward to the still almost meditative calm that he had come to expect after a normal weekend, and had been thinking how much he would enjoy the steady taking stock after the chaos, organised or otherwise, of Saturday. Ordinarily, he would be able to lose himself in the detail of the task, clipboard in hand, highlighter pen at the ready, making steady progress from left to right around the shelves. Barely had he completed the Humbrol carousel when the phone rang. This set the pattern for the morning. Every time it rang, he had to mark his place, put his clipboard, pen and highlighter carefully down, and pad over to the plinth. Ernest felt the interruptions every bit as keenly as Alan did, raising his head and following Alan's every move. He too had come to expect little interruption on a Monday morning, or indeed any morning, and was clearly mildly irritated by Alan's incessant walking about and noisy phone calls, breathing and sighing heavily when he re-settled himself to sleep.

Although Alan had, of course, to concentrate during these phone calls, he could not help surveying the state of the shop. The shelves and carousels yawned with gaps and the once neatly stacked boxes of kits were disarrayed and jumbled on the shelves and floor too. He found this lack of order difficult, but what he found more difficult was a rising sense of unease which he was choosing not to acknowledge. Luckily, he had plenty to occupy himself and buried himself in methodical tasks that restored order to his physical if not mental environment. Once he had a clear idea of what had been sold on Saturday, he settled down to order more stock and then answer the shop emails, in between more phone calls and several in-person shoppers. The mailbox was unnaturally full, 93 emails in the inbox rather than the usual 15 to 20, and it took him until well past 2 to get it all in hand and place new orders with the suppliers.

He felt he had earned himself a cup of tea and a biscuit, and sat wearily behind the plinth. He rested his elbows on the well-worn wood and blew gently on his tea, cupping the mug with both hands and staring into the middle distance. The unease within curled up to his surface and twined around the rising steam. Alan blew slightly more firmly, but the unease was determined to be seen. It misted up his glasses and forced him to put his mug down and reach deep into his pocket for a hanky. He took his glasses off, the left arm catching slightly against his ear, a tiny measure of his disquiet. He delved into his pocket, shook his hanky out and began to clear the misted lenses, taking his time to ensure the job was done properly, working his way into the crevices under the fine gold rims. He replaced his glasses, hoping to have banished the unease along with the steam, but to no avail. It was still very much there. He sighed, realising that despite his natural ability to push away uncomfortable thoughts, this unease was going to have to be looked at.

None of what had happened recently was normal. Martin had prepped him for normal, for unusual and even for the unexpected. They had gone over every scenario, but it had all been based on normal, and this wasn't the normal that Martin had left. Martin was in New Zealand. Martin was not here. Martin had not envisaged any of this - and Martin had envisaged most things. He had told Alan what to do in the event of fire, flood, burglary, biscuit purchasing and shoplifting, but he had not once mentioned that Alan should go rogue and organise a launch event for a product that he had no idea even existed. He had not said at any time, "D'you know what mate? Just change my entire way of doing things! Shake it up a bit!" He had not implied this in any way shape or form. Not one of the lever arch files that sat neatly shelved behind Alan's head contained information about what to do in the event of 476 customers in one day, or 50,000 likes on Instagram or needing to have a security guard.

Alan and Martin had agreed that Alan was to be in charge. No need for weekly catch-up calls or emails. Alan was in charge. Alan was to be trusted to run this shop because Martin trusted Alan. Nothing that Alan had ever done had led Martin to believe that he could not be trusted. Martin had gone to New Zealand for five weeks in the certain knowledge that when he returned, things would be exactly as he had left them. It had been very hard for Martin to let go, but once he had trusted Alan... and now Alan felt sick. Properly, really, sick. He pushed away his mug, watching the steam twirl and whirl and acknowledging the root cause of the unease. A small voice inside piped up, "But surely he will be pleased that sales are up by 4000%, or whatever ..." The very fact that the voice lacked specific figures was enough to convince Alan that it held no truth and the voice dwindled away.

Underhand. That was the word that sprang to mind now. The whole thing was underhand. He had not okayed any of this with Martin because he knew that it would not be okay. It was a deep affront to all that Martin had built up over the years. The things that Martin held dear, his customer base, his stock, his way of doing things, even the shop layout, were as they were because that's how Martin wanted them. And in agreeing to run the shop for five weeks, Alan was not only agreeing with Martin's way of doing things, he was also praising Martin for keeping the old ways going. Alan saw now that if Martin had wanted to change the shop in any way he would already have done so, and he could only ever view what Alan had done as a deep and personal criticism.

Alan felt sick all over again. Closing time could not come quickly enough.

Chapter 30

By the following day, Alan had largely been able to repackage the unease he had experienced and file it carefully under the category of 'things he'd rather not think about.' This was a category with a huge amount of diversity, ranging from the unfathomable depth of the loss of Robert through to Claire's state of happiness and his issues with the butcher. There was plenty to do in the shop and there seemed to be even more orders coming in than there had been the previous day.

One or two customers came and went and he ate his lunch whilst leafing through a trade magazine. There was great mention of the Nationals in Telford and he felt glad and proud that Nathan would be going and being part of it. The IPMA certainly knew how to run a good event and if it was anything like the time he had been about 15 years ago, it would definitely please Nathan, and Troy too of course. He had known Troy's dad Andy from way back, and they were a nice family. He couldn't remember what she was called, maybe Allison? He could picture her, but no name was forthcoming. Anyway. He knew that Nathan and Troy were slightly peeved that little Daisy would be coming too, but she always seemed like a nice sensible person to Alan and he thought they would all have a good time. Andy was taking the caravan and had booked on a site about 15 minutes away from the conference centre. Troy had shown them pictures on his phone as they'd been there last year too and it was surprisingly rural, with chickens tatting about and lots of trees and open space. When Alan had gone, he'd stayed at the Travelodge, which had met and even slightly exceeded his expectations, but he could see that the caravan option would better suit the children. It would be Nathan's first time staying in a caravan. With Claire being on her own, they had stuck to all-inclusive package holidays on alternate years, with Alan discreetly supporting financially in the background.

Claire had wanted the boys to have good holiday memories, 'like she had,' she had rather gratifyingly said, and their largely absent father had so far not offered them anything more glamorous than a fortnight with him in Milton Keynes. Perhaps if things had been different and they'd been together still, they'd have had their own caravan.

*

Alan and Jackie had been natural caravaners of course, buying their first 'van when the children were seven and five respectively. Alan had pushed for one long before that point but Jackie had held her ground and refused to be taking babies and toddlers, saying she couldn't countenance going away with anybody that wasn't in full control of their own bladder or bowels, and Robert had still been having occasional wet beds until he was nearly six. Claire of course had pretty much potty trained herself and he could never remember her having any kind of accident of that kind at all, so if it hadn't been for Robert they could have been caravanning years before.

They had bought their first caravan, after much perusing of Exchange and Mart, from a couple near Stevenage who had come into some money and were upgrading. Alan always thought it was important to know the reason for a sale and until he was satisfied that their story was plausible and did not conceal some massive flaw that the caravan possessed he was unwilling to commit. Its only flaw was that it was basic, and when they eventually went to see it on a sunny Saturday morning, they were thrilled. Alan went over every inch of it with a torch, notebook and pen, and Jackie opened and closed drawers and cupboards whilst keeping half an eye on the children, left sitting in the back of the car. The seller had been dubious about the capacity of Alan's Morris Marina for towing, instantly noting the lack of a tow bar, but Alan was able to reassure him that he had done his homework and was satisfied that she had the necessary power. Not wishing to rush ahead or spend money unnecessarily, Alan had decided not to have a tow bar fitted until he had actually bought a caravan, a decision he would come to regret. The deal was struck and they agreed that Alan would come and collect the caravan the following Friday evening, as the seller's driveway would need to be cleared to accommodate their bigger, better caravan, arriving on Saturday morning.

Alan arranged with the garage to have the tow bar fitted and what with ordering the parts, the earliest they could do it was Wednesday. Wednesday turned into Thursday and then Friday, and by 2 o'clock it became clear that the work was not going to be done on time. Alan could still now remember the frustration and shame he felt in having to phone and explain that he would not be able to collect the caravan after all. The sellers had been very nice about it though and the man had offered, partly through kindness and partly because he wanted the damn thing off his driveway, to deliver it early the following morning. Despite everything, it had been a proud moment when the caravan was finally backed up, unhitched and theirs. The children had instantly swarmed over it, enchanted by the fold-up beds and the tiny fridge whilst Jackie had pottered about placing little bits and pieces in the cupboards and drawers. She had quietly been collecting things for the caravan and was able to put in a new potato peeler, four plastic glasses and some artificial flowers in a vase to her satisfaction before setting to with the tape measure. She was a skilled seamstress and it was nothing to her to run up some new curtains. She had made a lovely job of the curtains he'd thought; co-ordinating them with the paintwork of the car was a nice detail of the sort Alan appreciated. Jackie had insisted on calling it yellow, but it was officially known as 'Sandglow' and sat somewhere between orange, yellow and beige. You really didn't see that colour anymore, but it had been quite a bold choice at the time and the kids had loved it from the start, bouncing about on the beige ('Sorrel' actually) back seat, shrieking when their little bare legs stuck to the hot vinyl. Robert always wanted the arm rest down but Claire didn't, preferring to be able to slide about and 'accidentally' squash Robert as the car turned a corner in the days before rear seatbelts came in. They both knew it annoyed their father to draw on the hurred up windows, but they did it anyway, tittering and daring each other to write the word 'bum'. He'd make them clean the windows properly afterwards with a cloth and polish if they did it, but they still did it anyway, little tinkers that they were.

As soon as the tow bar was fitted to everyone's satisfaction, there was no stopping them. Almost every weekend they'd be off somewhere, never terribly far but they were happy times. Idly, Alan started to Google 'camp sites near Telford' and quickly shocked himself with the discovery that the campsite nearest to the International Centre was a naturist site! He blushed and immediately closed the laptop. He pulled himself together and re-opened the laptop. Could this be the site that Andy planned to take Nathan to? Surely not, but he felt duty bound to investigate. The wide open spaces and shady woodlands could be anywhere, but there were no chickens in any of the pictures on the website. No naked people either, but he paled to think that they were there, and in November too. Another five minutes online gave him the reassurance he needed. A second campsite, a little further away, had a website heaving with chickens and family-friendly fun. Nathan would be safe.

Chapter 31

Nathan hovered in the gloomy hallway, fingers in his mouth, echoing his younger thumb-sucking years. His head was dropped low and he appeared to be looking at the bag at his feet. He wasn't.

"Nathan!" shouted Claire from the back door. "Are you coming, or what?" She waited, listening.

Nathan blinked and shifted his gaze to the bottom stair. The carpet was slightly worn at the tread and the small dark marks that peppered it bore witness to spills and stains, some of his own making. The bobbled weave of the carpet filled his gaze, giving his frantic brain something to focus on.

"Nathan? Where are you?" Claire's exasperation was clear. She listened again. Nothing. "Oh for pity's sake, " she huffed, kicking off her shoes and jangling her keys. "Nathan?" She called again, thinking him to be far away, upstairs or perhaps even gone out. She stomped through the kitchen, flicking the light on as she went. She flung open the door to the hallway and shocked herself by discovering him standing, frozen, in mid stare. He made himself fractionally smaller, but other than that he made no indication that he knew she was there. Perhaps he didn't. Claire matched his stillness, only the bulk and rustle of her outdoor clothes intruding on the moment.

She looked, really looked at her boy. He was pale, for sure, but he often was. He was dressed and ready to go but he clearly wasn't ready.

"What's going on Nathan?", her voice echoing the deep concern and love she felt for her youngest child, "what is it, hey?"

Nothing, no response at all. Claire shuffled round him and hefted herself on to the second stair. It had been so long since the last time this had happened, but clearly, she hadn't forgotten what to do. Like putting on an old friend of a coat on the first chilly day after a long hot summer, Claire settled in and began.

"So, I can see you're struggling, Nathan. Looks like you're finding this hard."

Nathan's fists rippled fractionally, the only acknowledgement that he had heard her at all.

"Okay, it's okay. We can do this together. I'm here. It's alright." She paused and shifted her weight on the stair. He flicked his eyes towards the noise but immediately returned them to the stair below her.

"Okay, so, it's okay, we've got plenty of time. You haven't got to be there until 5.30 and it's only 5 now. Plenty of time. Looks like you've packed your bag, got everything you need." She looked at the bag at his feet and moved it marginally with her toe. His knees tightened.

"I've already put your model in the car. In the boot, nice and safe in the box, all wrapped and packed by Grandad."

At the mention of his name, Nathan's eyes widened very slightly. Claire noticed, and went on, encouraged.

"He came round earlier, to wish you well, but you weren't quite back from school. He couldn't stay, I guess you know why?" Nathan could hear the amusement and love in her voice and turned his head to meet her gaze.

"Yes, that blooming dog! Nowhere near feeding time, but he's whistling and leaping all over the place, getting under Grandad's feet so much that in the end, he just gave in and took him home to feed him." Claire told it as if she could see it and so Nathan could too. He cleared his throat and swallowed, but no other sound left him.

"I expect he'll be done by now. He won't want to have missed you. I wonder if I should give him a call?"

Nathan, still wordless, edged a little nearer to Claire. She fumbled for her phone among her layers of clothing, finally dragging it out and scrolling to find Alan's number.

"Tell him to come. And bring Ernest." He spoke so quietly he almost didn't speak at all.

Alan answered almost immediately and they could hear that he was breathless.

"Hello?"

"Hi Dad. It's Claire." She tried to catch Nathan's eye - a joke between them that Grandad was the only person in the world who never looked at the name of the caller before answering, but it was too soon.

"Oh, Claire, I'm just out with the dog, can I call you back?'

"No, wait, Dad, can you come over? We haven't left yet and Nathan, we, he wants to see Ernest before he goes."

"And him," breathed Nathan.

"And you, he says!" added Claire jovially, belying the relief she felt flooding her like a spring tide.

"Does he now? Alright, I'm not far away."

He ended the call and left Claire looking at the phone in her hand.

"Well, that's good isn't it? Sit down with me while we wait?"

He let the words hang in the air. He breathed in, then turned and sat heavily on the bottom stair.

"Going away is hard, isn't it?" Claire began. "Especially when you've been looking forward to it so much."

Nathan didn't respond but she could feel him listening.

"You know we had a caravan when I was little? We used to go all over in it. So much packing up to do, getting all the things you think you might need, we used to drive Gran mad, getting under her feet and eating stuff she'd just packed." She smiled at the memory and leant gently in to Nathan's shoulder. "You're going to have a great time, with Troy and Daisy." At the mention of her name, Nathan shot her a look that suggested Daisy was not going to be part of the great time. Claire laughed, "Oh, she's alright, and she thinks the world of you. And anyway, you and Troy will be so busy setting up your exhibits and seeing what everyone else has got and looking at all the stalls, there won't be time for her to annoy you."

"I guess. It's just…"

Claire waited. The silence expanded. Nathan shifted his weight and twisted towards her.

"What if, what if, I miss you and I cry and I …"

Claire reached down and scooped him up, pulling his too-bigness into her arms. She let him cry and held the back of his head, cradling the hard bone of his skull beneath his too-long hair.

"Oh my boy! I know, it's alright. We'll miss each other, but you'll be having so much fun you won't even… it's okay, it's okay."

At that moment, they heard Alan's voice at the back door, left open by Claire. "Anybody home?" he called. Nathan's head bobbed up and he smeared his face with his coat sleeve. He met Claire's eyes but had no more time to do anything except shelter from the frantic skittering of Ernest, beyond pleased to find not one but two of his favourite people unexpectedly low to the ground. Within moments, Nathan and the little dog were rolling about on the floor, all Nathan's tears but a salty memory on Ernest's tongue.

"Everybody okay?" said Alan slowly as he came round into the dark hallway.

Claire wiped her eyes and stood up. "Yes, all good, we're just getting his stuff in the car then I'm going to pop him round there. Glad you got here in time," she understated.

Nathan struggled to his feet, finding himself between Alan and his mother. He wrapped his arms tightly around Alan, who gave only the tiniest surprised hesitation before wrapping him right back.

"Bye Grandad. I love you."

"I love you too, Nathan." He nodded at Claire, understanding what had gone on with a tenderness and gentleness that set Claire off again.

"Oh blimey," she said. "Come on you, let's get you in the car. You coming too Dad?"

"Yes, he is, aren't you Grandad? Can you?"

"I don't see why not."

They gathered Nathan's bag, and Claire ushered them out of the back door, turning lights off as she went. She locked the door, and turned to watch them struggling themselves, the bag and the dog into the car, lit by the glow of the street lamp. She smiled. It would be okay.

Chapter 32

It was okay. It was more than okay. Nathan received a rapturous welcome from Troy and Daisy, who were doubly thrilled and surprised to see Ernest tumbling out of the car. Alan was greeted warmly by Andy, who immediately took Alan, at his request, to see the caravan. It was packed and ready to go on the driveway and the two men straight away stood in time-honoured fashion, hands in pockets pointing with their heads at interesting features Andy wished to share. Alan remarked that things had moved on since his day and marvelled at the automatic hitching system and neatness of the toiletting arrangements. Andy seemed pleased and had just offered to show Alan his workshop when Allison (Alan had been right) came out of the kitchen drying her hands on a tea towel. She greeted Claire warmly and said that she expected she was looking forward to a bit of peace and quiet without the kids, because she certainly was, at which point Claire burst into tears. Allison awkwardly hustled Claire back into the kitchen, clutching the tea towel and moving towards the kettle.

"Let's get you a cup of tea, shall we?' she suggested, gesturing to Claire to take a seat at the scrubbed pine kitchen table whilst picking up the kettle and taking it to the sink.

"I'm so sorry, it's ridiculous," snuffled Claire, scrabbling about in her coat pockets for a tissue before she sat down heavily. The tissue she found was very much past its best and began crumbling in Claire's hand. Allison tactfully noticed this and put a box of tissues down at Claire's elbow.

"Oh, thank you, I'm so sorry," she repeated.

"Nothing to be sorry for at all," replied Allison, reaching for mugs, tea, sugar and milk in quick succession, "I cry all the time. Famous for it! Can't get through an episode of *Heartbeat* without weeping! I ask you, *Heartbeat!*"

Claire gave a huff of laughter through her tears.

"I used to love *Heartbeat*! Is it even on anymore?" She raised her gaze to Allison.

"Well, there was a time when it was never off, 18 series or something like that, but I got the bug, and now, lucky me, I have Series 1-7 'The Rowan Years' on a 29 Disc box set! Andy gave me a spice rack for Christmas, so I went out and bought it myself in January."

Claire laughed in spite of herself.

"29 disc box set! How far through are you?"

"Life has somewhat got in the way, I admit, but I'm cracking on, and I'm on disc 2 currently. The kids only have to hear the opening bars of the theme tune and it's like Pavlov's dogs, except instead of salivating they disappear upstairs. Result!"

Claire took the tea that Allison was holding out and smiled up to her. She thanked her and cradled the mug with both hands.

"Biscuit?" Allison offered, holding out a slightly battered tin half full of slightly wonky biscuits. "Daisy made them, but I can guarantee that hygiene standards were high. If Troy had made them, that would be a different matter."

"Does he do much baking then?"

"Sometimes, but he'd rather be modelling. Of course! Like his dad! Daisy's the baker, bless her. Always asking for bizarre ingredients. Just before bed, usually. She put Pandan extract on my shopping list last week. I did ask for it at Sainsbury's in town, but they looked at me as if I was asking for crack cocaine, so I think they didn't have it."

"What is it? I've never heard of it."

"Oh, it's a sort of Asian flavouring she's seen on *Bake Off*. It's green and tastes like, well, more of a perfume sort of, hard to explain. Anyhow, it's green and you can get it from the Chinese Supermarket near Stevenage, which we did, but apparently now she needs a special tin, which we don't have, so Project Pandan is on hold, for now, I guess. So anyway, what are you up to this weekend? Is your older boy at home, Mark is it?"

'Matt. No, he's just moved up to Explorers - the one after Scouts? And he's gone off on some weekend adventure..." Claire struggled for the right word, "...weekend?"

Allison nodded encouragingly, reaching for a biscuit herself then pushing the tin towards Claire.

"Yes, so it's just me at home. So, not sure really. Clear out the airing cupboard?"

Allison looked at Claire, unsure if this was humour or reality.

"Clear out the airing cupboard? Big job is it?"

Claire laughed, shaking her head.

"No, probably have it done in half an hour. I haven't really had time to think what I'll do, it's been mad busy at work this week."

"Hmm, what do you do? Nathan wasn't sure, just that you travelled."

"Ha! That makes it sound glamorous. No, I work for a medical supplies company, and we have clients all over. Sometimes..." She paused for dramatic effect. "I go as far as Yarmouth!"

"Oooh, get you! Travelling to The Far East! I like it!"

Claire laughed again. "I'll remember to use that phrase next time I go."

"Still, I bet it's never the same, is it, being on the road, different clients?"

"Yes, there is that, but," Claire sighed, "sometime the driving gets me down, you know, and it's, well. What about you? What do you do?"

"Oh, well, I'm only part time these days, but I'm a call handler for the Police."

"Oh wow! That's amazing! Is that what you've always done?" asked Claire, leaning forward.

"Well, the last 15 years or so I have. Before that I just did temping, secretarial stuff."

"Big difference! So, how do you manage with the shifts? I mean, is it like Police shifts, or more, you know, 9-to-five?"

"No, it's all flexible working, sometimes nights, weekends you know. But Andy and I have always juggled it between us. He works from home a lot and I used to be full time, before kids, but I'm down to a point 4 week now, which is okay. Full on, but okay! So, for me to be 'home alone' and not working this weekend, well, it's like winning the lottery!"

"You didn't fancy going with them then? To Telford?"

Allison gave her a look that merely touched on how much she would not have wanted to go to the IPMS Scale ModelWorld event in Telford.

Claire laughed again, and took a sip of her tea before putting it down on the table.

"So, I mean, I hope you don't mind my asking, but how do you get into being a call handler?"

"Oh, I had a boyfriend at the time who was a Police Officer. I had literally no idea it was an actual job, but you know, it's…" she paused, realising that she had misunderstood the question, noticing that Claire was hanging on her every word, "hang on a minute, sorry, you said do, not did. Are you thinking of it for yourself?"

Claire drew in a big breath, lifting her eyebrows at the boldness of herself, "Yes, yes, I am." She blushed and looked down at her tea. "Well, yes, maybe. I mean, maybe Police Officer or PCSO, or, I don't know, but yes, a career in the Police. It's what I always wanted, before, you know, 'life got somewhat in the way'. So, yes."

"Claire! That is so cool! What stage of the process are you at?"

Before Claire could reply, Daisy came bowling into the kitchen, shouting out as she ran.

"Mu-um! Troy says I can't take Mr Snuffles with me!"

"What? It's not anything to do with Troy. Of course you can take him."

"He says I can't. He says he smells and if I take him he's going to throw him out of the window," Daisy went on, her voice quivering with righteous indignation, her hands clutching the off-grey rabbit-shaped cloth lump to her chest. She stuck her chin down and buried her face in the saggy toy. Claire and Allison exchanged looks. Allison got up and put one arm around the truculent child.

"Come on Daisy-do, let's go and sort that brother of yours out shall we?"

Daisy allowed herself a frisson of satisfaction before remembering she was supposed to be very very sad and reburying her head in Mr Snuffles.

By the time that Mr Snuffles was safely on board the caravan and Ernest had been removed from it not once but twice, it was almost 6.15. Claire, Allison and Alan stood on the driveway waving until the rear of the caravan disappeared as it turned right at the end of the road, joining the weekend traffic northbound. As one, their gaze turned to Ernest, at the very end of his lead, peeing against a plant pot by the door. He had obviously been holding on for some time.

"Blimey, Ernest," said Claire, watching the torrent pooling and then snaking over the block paving and into the road.

"I'm so sorry," said Alan, powerless to move the dog mid pee.

"It's fine," said Allison, and meant it.

Eventually, Ernest finished and was dragged away by Alan.

"So sorry, I'd better be getting off. Thanks Allison. See you on Tuesday, Claire?"

"Yes, Dad, see you then," she replied, pushing her hands deep into her coat pockets, waiting for him to go, then turning to Allison, "Thanks for the tea, and, you know, anyway, I'd better be getting off too. Thanks Allison."

"Not so fast Chief Inspector! I've got a bottle of wine and an episode of *Heartbeat* wants watching. Care to join me?"

"Oh, that's very kind, but I couldn't, I mean, it's your…" but Allison wouldn't let her finish.

"Listen, there's not that many people around that like *Heartbeat*, and anyway, I want to hear more about your plans. Girl Power! Us women have got to stick together. Come on, that wine won't drink itself."

"Well, okay, a small glass, I guess, thank you, that'd be lovely."

And just like that, Claire was another step closer to the thin blue line.

Chapter 33

Sunday had its own pattern in Alan's house, moving gently around Ernest's needs and Alan's habits. He had always liked to walk to the shop and collect his paper and a Twix, and when Jackie had been alive, he'd brought home a *Radio Times* and a Wispa too.

This was a ritual which Ernest enjoyed and the shopkeeper was happy for him to come in to the shop, especially after he'd had complaints about Ernest's furious barking when tied up outside. Alan passed one or two people he knew well enough to say hello to, and one or two that he gave a friendly, but not too friendly, head nod to. He certainly found he knew more people now that he had the dog, and Ernest had made his own friends too. 'Friends' was perhaps pushing it - rather, people he identified as having the time to fuss him or even better, people who went around with dog treats in their pockets. Other dogs he was less bothered about. He didn't feel it was a problem, he certainly wasn't aggressive, just not interested. When off lead in the park, he would go about his business, deeply involved in finding what might have been dropped, but showing clear disdain for the exuberant and happy-go-lucky dogs that zoomed near or past him. Occasionally, a puppy - always a puppy - not having learnt to read the subtle signs of a dog who does not, under any circumstances, want to play, would bound up to him, bowing and wagging in front of him. He would sneeze, then solidly bark until the bewildered youth got the message or lost interest.

Alan took his paper and Twix to the counter and laid them down, the better to find the exact money in his pocket, whilst still holding Ernest's lead quite tightly. He didn't altogether believe that Ernest might not disgrace himself (theft or toilet-wise) and Ernest resented both the tightness of the lead and the lack of trust. He made a rather pointed choking icky noise which Alan chose to ignore, but nonetheless speeded up his search for change, the quicker to get out in case Ernest was actually going to produce something. The shopkeeper peered over the counter to see if kitchen paper and a spray needed to be offered, but leant back again, satisfied that it was only a dry cough.

"Keeping well, Alan?" he said as he scanned the barcodes.

"Oh well, can't complain. Thank you. And you?"

"Yes, ticking on. I hear things are going very well up at the shop. My niece was full of it, couple of Saturday's ago, was it?"

"Yes, oh, yes, the launch. Last week. Yes, it was certainly a much bigger event than we anticipated. Still busy now, in fact."

"Good for you. Enjoy your day."

"Thank you, yes, and you." replied Alan, gathering up his paper and his Twix and dragging Ernest out of the open door. The clouds overhead retained their earlier solid intensity and looked no nearer to producing rain than they had before, so he decided to stick to his usual practice and head off to the park. The shopkeeper had inadvertently fuelled Alan's unease and sent him off on a train of thought that was hurtling towards Martin's return and silent unexpressed fury and hurt at what he had done to the shop. Sales had been up again, and whilst it might be possible to conceal the launch from Martin, clear profits would very hard to explain.

Alan's usual bench was free, well away from the pond and near enough to the cafe and toilet block for both to be accessible, if necessary, but still worth the little walk uphill from the path. The paper was full of the usual outrage surrounding Brexit, awful politicians and a smattering of horrific accidents and teens gone wrong as well as a long article about how to make your money work for you which made him feel guilty again, but unfortunately, the wind had now picked up considerably, making it impossible for him to control the pages, and so he reluctantly folded up the paper and partially sat on it whilst he ate his Twix. He was well into the final third of the second bar when his attention was drawn to a lady in a white coat waving at him and walking up the slope towards him.

"Alan!"she called breathily. "I thought it was you!" He experienced a stomach drop that sent his brain into red mist panic mode. Who on earth was this woman? Did he know her? She knew his name, so clearly, she knew him, which sent his anxiety levels up even further. She continued striding towards the bench, jute shopping bag on one crooked elbow held tightly to her padded mid length jacket. The wind was blowing her hair about, and she used her other hand to keep it out of her eyes, shading her face as he did so and hampering Alan even further from recognising her. She was getting closer now and still, nothing.

"How are you? So lovely to see you've still got the dog," she turned and called out, "Ernest! Hey, Ernest, come here, how are you?" Ernest looked up briefly, gave her the canine equivalent of a chin tilt, and carried on his survey of the bin area by the cafe.

"Oh, he's a tinker, isn't he? He's always been a bit rude. Lovely, but rude."

The lady was throwing down clues for Alan now, but his brain couldn't work fast enough to follow them up. She clearly knew Ernest, and well too, judging by her accurate assessment of him.

"Oh yes, he is, absolutely!" Alan smiled in a way that he hoped conveyed recognition, but clearly failed.

"How's Martin getting on?" So, she knew Martin, she knew Ernest, but still, he had no idea who she was. His instinct said "bluff."

"Good, yes. In New Zealand! Not due back till just before Christmas."

"Yes, I thought so. I see him on Facebook, posting all the time, the pictures from Rotorua were amazing! He'll be having the time of his life. I love New Zealand!"

She was clearly party to detailed information about Martin's movements, but who was she?

"Oh, have you been?" suggested Alan, hoping she might drop some more nuggets he could use to place her.

"Yes, Keith and I went for our 25th wedding anniversary, I'd go back like a shot, but, well, you know.'

Alan didn't. Not at all. He was working furiously through his mental Rolodex now. Who the hell was Keith? Did he even know anyone called Keith? Who had been to New Zealand? The strain was clearly beginning to show on his face now. The lady fixed him with a steady look.

"I'm Carol? Joan's neighbour? How is she by the way? I must pop and see her again soon."

This just got worse. Who the hell was Joan? Alan played for time and dropped his Twix.

"Oh, where's that gone? Must find it before Ernest does," he said, dropping down to look below the slatted seat of the bench.

Carol bustled round to the back of the bench, trilling out, "It's here, I've got it!"

Alan misunderstood and began reaching from the front of the bench, his stretched fingers almost dislocating his shoulder in their efforts to do anything rather than be exposed as not recognising this person.

She bent down and picked it up lightly, a move Alan was not expecting. He withdrew at speed, scraping his other shoulder on the bench as he went.

"Oooh, that looked sore," winced Carol. "Are you alright? I think that was my fault, I'm so sorry."

Alan now added pain to his confusion. It didn't help to clear his mind.

She watched him struggle awkwardly to his knees and back on to the bench.

"Oh no, your paper!" she pointed to his side.

He looked done in, but was sufficiently aware to be able to slap his hand down on the paper, trapping the pages before they built up enough momentum to lift and separate away across the park.

The lady had the grace to look ruffled herself and held on to her hair as it slapped about her face, which was full of concern for Alan. A kind lady, anyway, even if he had no clue who she was. Or Keith. Or Joan. Joan! Martin's mother-in- law! This spurred him on.

"So, you know Joan, do you?"

She gave him a slightly puzzled look. "Yes, I've lived next door to Joan for maybe, ooh, fifteen years now. Well, not anymore I suppose, now she's at Foxholes!"

Foxholes! Thank the Lord. Carol! He'd met her at Foxholes! He'd been there with Martin and Ernest and she'd just been leaving. She lived next door to Martin's mother-in-law Joan, Ernest's legal owner. Of course!

"Of course! Where I met you! With Martin! And Ernest!" Carol was good enough not to make a thing of it, but she could see that he did now know who she was, but blatantly hadn't until just a moment ago.

"Foxholes, eh?" he continued, "Yes, that's where Joan is. She seems happy enough there, I think."

"It's a nice enough place, beautiful grounds. My cousin was there in the spring, just went in for respite, but he's full of its praises. Lots going on, he says. He's started volunteering there now, visiting some of the oldies, you know. I think you might know him, he's into model making - Stephen Allerton?"

Alan's heart sank. His brain just wasn't up to this.

"Er, Stephen Allerton? Ummm ..." he touched his chin to suggest he was thinking, but clearly wasn't.

She ploughed on.

"Stephen Allerton? Tallish chap, grey hair, glasses?"

This really didn't narrow things down. She was describing approximately 78% of Alan's model-making acquaintants.

She continued.

"Stephen Allerton? Used to work in construction. Drives a Prius? Lives up by Tesco's?"

Nothing.

"Oh, you do know Stephen," she smiled and nodded encouragingly.

"Tesco Metro's in town?" Alan frowned. He couldn't think of any residential properties near there at all, let alone someone he knew who lived there.

"No, Tesco's on the bypass."

Realisation dawned.

"Steve! Steve Allerton! Fancy that. Oh yes, Steve and I go way back. Nice man. I had heard he hadn't been well, but he's okay now?"

"Yes, all good. He had a big back op, and you know Anne's only tiny, so she couldn't manage him at home."

Alan was by now on a roll. He knew that Steve was married to Anne and that Anne was indeed miniature.

"Of course, no, I can see that," and he really could.

Alan was flooded with relief that he had been so successful in his ID skills, and, quite buoyed up, got to his feet and said, "I was thinking of getting a coffee from the cafe, can I get you one?"

She paused for only the shortest of beats before replying, "Yes, why not? That'd be lovely, thank you."

Chapter 34

"So, what do you think?" Nathan looked around the table, trying to gauge their thoughts from their faces.

Claire had finished eating and tipped her head to one side, looking up to a section of Magnolia-covered wall above the beige and pine trim of the kitchen cabinets. Thinking required a non-cluttered visual for her and Nathan knew this. Alan was harder to read, as he was still chasing the last of his pork stroganoff around his plate.

"Grandad?" Nathan nudged, "what do you think?"

Alan settled his knife and fork carefully together, leant back on his chair and pushed his glasses back up his nose.

"I appreciate, and admire, the research you have done, and I don't see why it shouldn't be perfectly possible."

Nathan reached for the air above him in victory, both fists balled in joy as he then drew them back into his body with a loud, "Yessss!"

Alan immediately raised both his flat open palms to Nathan in what he hoped was a gesture of acknowledgement.

"But..."

Nathan froze.

"But...I don't see how we can host it at the shop."

"Grandad! We had 476 people going through on launch day. We've only got to have 251 and the record will be ours! An actual world record! How amazing would that be, Grandad? Troy's dad knows someone who works at Airfix, we could totally do this. All the people I talked to about it at Telford said they'd definitely come. It would be so cool, don't you think Grandad? Mum?"

Claire had dropped her gaze to the table. She focused now on the smooth veneer chestnut-brown surface, something she had done all her life. Its grain and pattern were as familiar to her as her own hands. Her mother used to pull her up on it - Claire, stop staring at the table! - but Alan understood that she was processing something.

"The thing is, Nathan," said Alan, intervening to allow Claire more thinking time, "it's a super idea. I mean, what a wonderful idea! Setting a new world record for the most number of people constructing aircraft models, who wouldn't want to be involved in that?"

"So, why not Grandad? We could do it at the shop!"

Alan's unease that had been bubbling fiercely in the pit of his stomach finally over-boiled.

"We just can't. I can't. Martin left me in charge of his shop and look what I've done to it! I've made it a magnet for teenagers, the shop is permanently full of youths discussing ...sprue cutters, there's never a moment's peace in there, the ordering alone takes me a whole morning, stock's out faster than I can get it in, the website's broken twice through sheer volume of traffic and if I hear that door ping one more time, I think I'm going to go bonkers."

There was a stunned silence.

"Blimey," said Claire.

Alan removed his glasses and squeezed his eyes hard with both hands. Nobody moved.

"I'm okay, I'm okay," exhaled Alan, replacing his glasses and breathing in. "I just can't go on deceiving Martin like this any more. It's just not right."

Claire and Nathan exchanged baffled glances.

"Dad? What are you talking about?"

"Martin is going to be so angry at what I've done, quite rightly so. He left me in charge of his business because he trusted me, and see how I repaid him. Wrecked what he built up over 20 years!"

"Dad, what are you saying? I don't understand. Has the business gone under?"

Alan laughed bitterly. "Ha, no, exactly the opposite. It's bringing in more money every week. Takings have never been this high. It's going to put Martin into a whole new tax bracket. Oh God."

"So, I still don't understand. Dad?"

"Martin left me in charge of something he loved and had built exactly like he wanted it. I've just come along and changed everything. He's going to think I don't respect his life's work. He'll see it as the ultimate criticism. Oh God."

"Oh, Dad, no, no he doesn't. He really doesn't."

Alan looked up, horrified. "He knows?? Oh my God. How does he know? He's in New Zealand."

"Dad, he knows, and he's delighted. Couldn't be happier, he's over the moon. How could he not be?"

"What are you saying Claire? Did you phone him? Did *he* phone *you*? We agreed we wouldn't phone. Why did he phone you? He could have phoned me, he knew that."

"Dad, Dad, stop. Nathan, show him? It's been all over Facebook. Everyone's been sharing it, everyone! He's even made a Facebook page for the shop, loads of people follow it, he's loving it."

The idea of Martin 'loving it' made everyone feel a little embarrassed, but they let it pass.

"Look Grandad! Look at what he's said, here. He's really pleased. Look. Look at this one, he's even tagged you in, but you're not on Facebook, so... but Grandad, he's really really pleased! Look, oh, wait, that's, no, he's talking about his sky dive there, but this one, see, he's really really really pleased!"

Alan gazed at Nathan's phone, as the boy scrolled through Martin's posts. He was right. Martin was really pleased.

The relief was instant, flooding over him like central heating after a week in a tent.

"So can we do it then Grandad? Do the world record attempt of the most people making a model in the shop? Can we?"

Claire stepped in. "Nathan it's a fantastic idea, it really is, but I'm thinking about how on earth we get over 250 people making their own individual model in the shop. That 476, they were passing through, they would need room, a bit of space, you know?"

"Your mother's right Nathan, it's just not big enough."

"Not just the shop, the car park too, we could put marquees up, Troy's dad's got one he said we could use. We'd get tables, and chairs too maybe, for the old people, from the Scout hut, he says."

"So Andy's on board then?" asked Alan.

"Yeah, he thinks it'd be great. He loves a World Record. They've got nearly every Guinness Book of World Records going back to, like, 1974," he paused, "or something. Anyway, yes, he really wants to do it too. He says he's got loads of contacts."

"I'm sure he has."

"It could work you know Dad. The car park's bigger than you'd think, especially once the lockable bollards are laid flat. We could probably get the bathroom shop on board too, use their allocated area, if we ask them well in advance. We might struggle with customer parking then of course and it'd cause chaos, a massive knock on effect on the High Street, if people don't observe the double yellows."

"Agreed. Well, Nathan, I'm not saying yes, and I'm not saying no. I think we should all go, Troy and Andy too, and have a jolly good look, when it's light and we can see what's what. Now, I could do Wednesday afternoon, early closing, but you'll all be working or at school, so it's going to have to be Saturday. I'll start floating the idea with a few people, local clubs and so on, gauge the interest a bit."

"Oh, there's interest alright Grandad. Loads of people at the show said they'd come. Troy and I reckon we should aim for at least 300."

Alan smiled, not just at his grandson's excited face, but at his enthusiasm and passion. It was a wonderful thing to witness, and now, now that he had been released from his unease, he was going to do everything he could, with Martin's blessing, to make this happen.

Chapter 35

Saturday came around, far too slowly for Nathan's liking, and by the time Andy and Troy arrived at the shop at 10 o'clock, Nathan was in a state of high excitement. Greetings were made and yet more synopses of the high points of Scale ModelWorld were exchanged. Alan knew that Nathan's entry hadn't won anything, which wasn't surprising for his first attempt, but Andy was able to report that it hadn't looked out of place among the other entries in the class and it was very much hoped that he would try again next year and have success then. Alan kindly asked Troy about his gold award and Troy kindly showed him lots of photos, from numerous different angles and perspectives. Everybody knew that Andy had won gold in not one but two classes and been runner up for National Champion, but it was Claire's first opportunity to hear about some of the more exciting Special Interest Groups displays that were exhibited, being particularly impressed and intrigued by the group name Film Fangs, devoted to horror and sci-fi in all its miniature forms. Once the talk turned to the many different retailer stands and insider gossip, Claire took the opportunity to excuse herself and crack on with her tape measure in the car park.

By the time Andy came out, she had come to an uncomfortable conclusion.

"I don't think it's going to work Andy. I'm reckoning that the Scout hall tables are, what, a metre and a half?"

Andy thought for a moment and then agreed.

She went on. "So, even allowing for, let's say, 50 cm per modeller, which is tight I'd say, there's no way we'd get more than 150 participants out here. Maybe another 25 in the shop? That still leaves us 76 people short of a world record."

Andy nodded. "I hear you, Claire, I do," he replied, hands deep in pockets and his thoughts clearly focussed on the available space, "I guess you've taken into account the dog-leg behind the bathroom shop?"

"Yes, yes, I have, and even supposing we could get rid of the wheelie bins for the day, which I don't know that we could, that would only give us another, what? Seven places? You couldn't have anyone at the end there, so near the fire door."

"I agree," he nodded, "I guess we'd better go on in and break the bad news. I'm not going to lie, I'm gutted, but those boys…" He shook his head slowly.

The shop was somewhat fuller than they had left it, as various teenagers were now loafing about by the decals display and Alan and the boys and Ernest were chatting to a number of more mature customers. Alan had taken the unprecedented step of offering hot drinks to non-family members and was a little flustered by his own boldness, but no longer hampered by the unease he threw caution to the wind and opened a packet of biscuits too. The teenagers (and Ernest) were drawn by the rustle of the opening packet and it soon became clear that an impromptu meeting was taking place.

Everybody looked and listened hard as Claire drew a plan of the shop and car park on the back of the life-size cutout figure of Avalar, and several sensible suggestions were made, but whichever way they looked at it, they couldn't get the numbers past 187, not nearly enough for a World Record Attempt. Everyone had total confidence that they would get enough people, it was just where they would put them.

The door pinged just as everyone was blowing on their coffee and racking their brains about how to configure the space differently. Alan looked over to see a tall older man with grey hair and glasses, accompanied by a lady of similar age wearing a white coat.

"Steve! Steve Allerton! Carol! How are you both?"

"Yes, good thank you Alan, yourself? Busy in here isn't it?"

Alan ignored him, full of delight to find that he could properly introduce these two people with their actual names.

"Everybody, this is Carol, who lives next door to Joan, Martin's mother-in-law, and her cousin Steve Allerton, who drives a Prius and lives up by Tesco's."

Everybody smiled and nodded a little awkwardly, except for Carol, who broke into a wide smile, and Andy, who said, "Tesco's in town? I didn't realise there was any residential property near there?"

Carol rolled her eyes at Alan, who rolled them right back. Steve explained that it was the Tesco's near the bypass, and Claire called what was now officially a meeting to order.

"So, everybody, we are all united in our wish to go ahead with the World Record Attempt for the most people making an aircraft in one place?"

Everybody nodded, except for one of the teenagers, who bravely stuck his hand in the air.

"Yes?" Claire fixed him with her gaze and got her clipboard ready to take notes.

"Er, yeah, I just, well, does it have to be an aircraft? Could it be, like, I dunno, a tank, or a spaceship, or something?"

Claire looked around to see if anybody had an opinion. They all looked directly at her. She was their leader.

"Thank you, yes, for this specific record attempt, it does specifically have to be an aircraft. We're aiming to beat the current record of 250 modellers, set I believe at RAF Hendon, so yes, it does have to be a plane. Aircraft. Thank you." Claire paused to see if there was further comment.

"So, aircraft. So, could it be a spaceship then? That's a type of aircraft, isn't it?" There was nodding among the teenagers and a gentle burr of noise. Claire sensed a challenge.

"In this instance, we will be sticking to the traditional sense of the word aircraft to eliminate the possibility of non-qualification due to complaints raised by the possibly disgruntled previous record holders."

Everybody mentally bowed before her. They needed this woman

to lead them.

"Okay, just asking, you know." He melted into the biscuits, beanie hat well down.

Claire went on, "So, we're agreed. We want to do this, but currently, we have no venue. Any thoughts anybody?"

The group blew on their coffees again, then one or two suggestions started to come forward. The library? The school? The school seemed the most likely option and Claire said that she would email the head to make some initial enquiries. Nathan and Troy began to mutter between themselves, not happy that their great idea should somehow become a school event. Troy was able to verbalise this, explaining how a similar thing had happened when the dog agility people had started to use the school hall on a Tuesday evening and before they knew it, Year 8's were being 'made' to help out in their school uniforms for D of E, which took all the fun out of it. Claire didn't see this as a valid argument and shut them down fairly quickly, saying that unless anybody else had any better ideas, this was the best chance they had. Everybody agreed, despite feeling a bit bad for Troy and Nathan, but at the same time not seeing how else it could be done. People were beginning to disperse, and so Alan was able to get over to where Steve and Carol were.

"So, Steve, I hear you're doing a bit of volunteering up at Foxholes?"

"Yes, yes, I am. In fact that's one of the reasons I've come in."

*

Twenty minutes later, Alan, buoyed up by a lack of unease and a tickling sensation that may have been a desire to impress Carol, was helping Steve to load his Prius with ten model kits, donated for free by the shop, for the benefit of Steve's new Model Club for Seniors, held every Tuesday at Foxholes. There was talk of some sort of advertising opportunity for the shop - 'The Model Shop proudly supports Foxholes' sort of thing -perhaps a feature for the local paper, all the usual gratitude when a small business supports its local community, and everybody felt good. Steve was hoping to draw in the wider community, not just residents and Carol had offered to make her Lemon Drizzle cake and bring it along. Alan explained that he would have liked to come, but of course he would be in the shop. If only it had been a Wednesday.

Carol brightened immediately.

"No reason it couldn't be a Wednesday, is there Steve?"

"Could be, no reason on my account. I'll have to check with Yvonne at Foxholes though. They've got Acro-dance one of the days and we wouldn't want to clash with that!" He huffed a laugh, imagining the lycra/glue-based chaos that might entail, "Although having said that, the room's probably big enough for all of us to be there at once!"

"Yes, that dining room, it used to be the ballroom I believe. It's beautiful really, French windows all along one side, straight on to the lawn, majestic Cedar tree to look at, slopes right down to the lake. Bit too much goose poo for my liking, but Ernest loves all that, don't you, cheeky?"

Ernest returned her gaze with a tolerant tail thump, whilst they all thought about the dining room at Foxholes, and how it might look filled with at least 251 eager modellers.

Chapter 36

Yvonne worked part time at Foxholes, organising entertainments and activities for the residents. She was good at her job, and the people she worked with knew they could rely on her as a cheerful and helpful member of the team. She was always immaculately dressed, in bright jewel colours, and everyone knew the sound of her little cloppy heels coming down the corridor. Her ability to plan and organise timetables and venues was rather taken for granted, but her office wall planner, with its colour-coding and post-it notes in pastel shades, merely hinted at the brilliance of her mind. She preferred to use post-it notes as they allowed her to be flexible and make short notice changes, a crucial part of her role and she had a specific brand that she ordered in from the States. Only last week, there'd been a last-minute death in the resident's lounge, which had of course been sad for the family of the deceased, but to Yvonne it was a juicy military-style operation to sensitively relocate 'Knit 'n' Natter' without upsetting or alarming anybody.

Yvonne was at her desk on Monday morning when the phone rang. She took longer to answer the phone than one would expect, given that it rested just a few centimetres from her right hand. She'd always loved costume jewellery and had a large and varied collection which she took great pleasure in choosing from each morning. Today's turquoise-centred Greek-inspired coin design earrings picked up the bright hue of her cropped jacket perfectly, but unfortunately they made it impossible to answer the phone. She took her time to unclip the back (she'd never had her ears pierced) and placed her right earring in a small porcelain dish (a souvenir from Xanthe) set ready by the phone for this express purpose. She answered with equal parts of efficiency and, she hoped, warmth. It was a tricky balance, being on the one hand reassuringly competent, yet on the other, not devoid of human compassion and willingness to compromise. She'd been working on this balance for nearly 30 years in her work life, and was happy that she had it about right. By the time she got home, however, she was pretty much out of pleasantness, having just enough left to cook the supper, hoover round and feed the cats, having long ago realised that you could have enough of people other than yourself. She liked people well enough, and was genuinely interested in helping them, but just not after 4.30. Or on Thursday, her day off.

Luckily for Steve, he chose to call her office first thing on Monday morning. She'd had a lovely weekend, going to a craft fair on Saturday and reading her book on Sunday and she was ready to knuckle down to work with a full tank of pleasantness. She listened carefully to Steve's request to move Seniors Model Club to Wednesday and immediately began moving post-it notes in her mind, thinking how it could be done. She told Steve she would get back to him and as soon as she'd put the phone down and replaced her earring, she started moving post-its for real. It turned out to be almost disappointingly straightforward, requiring an initial move by Crafty Card Making. They'd been angling for a day change for a while, complaining that their current Friday afternoon slot was marred by the aroma of fish pie in the hall. They would happily take the Tuesday morning slot currently occupied by Seniors Model Club. Tony, from Sing with Tony, had been moaning and saying how hard it was to motivate everyone first thing on a Monday morning, and she knew straight away that he would jump at the chance to ride the Friday-Afternoon-Feeling wave with the younger members of staff. That would free up Monday morning for Scrabble Club, the current Wednesday afternoon booking, all of whom were early birds anyway, and spent a lot of time muttering about 'keeping their brains sharp, not like some other people they could mention', despite finding it hard to stay awake after lunch, just like everybody else. Yvonne stood back and admired the new pattern of peach, mint and lilac post-its with satisfaction, and removing her turquoise earring again she phoned Steve back with the good news. She spent the rest of the morning re-typing the timetable, printing numerous copies in appropriate fonts and sizes, adding clip art where appropriate, printing, re-laminating and displaying the new timetables and emailing staff about the changes. Nobody need say they had not been told.

Tony was perhaps the most pleased with the changes and immediately went out to the stores shed to see if he still had any maracas. He was delighted to find that he did and began straightaway compiling a Calypso Favourites program that started with *Island in the Sun*, meandered through *Islands in the Stream* and finished with a rousing *Banana Boat Song*. He was a big Harry Belafonte fan but had always known that he could never get the required audience participation to successfully negotiate the call and response element of this classic on a Monday morning. He pictured residents clapping and responding to his dulcet tones with 'Daylight come and we wanna go home' and wondered if, for once, it might actually be worth hanging up his glitter ball. Sadly for Tony, Yvonne vetoed this last song, fearing it might cause some sort of rebellion among the more disgruntled residents and he had to settle for *Three Little Birds*. Still a crowd pleaser, but not the same.

*

Steve relayed the good news to Alan, and also offered to pick him up from the shop on Wednesday lunchtime. Alan thanked him, but explained that he couldn't impose on Steve's kindness, as he would have Ernest with him, and would travel in his own vehicle to Foxholes, where he planned to park Ernest with Joan for the duration of the club.

Steve was unfazed by the idea of transporting Ernest and immediately suggested a blanket on the backseat. He pointed out that although he generally found the Prius to be a satisfactory car, it had very little rear seat room, which in this case was an advantage as it would better contain Ernest and stop him wandering about. Alan was beginning to be swayed by this proposal, as he very much wanted to experience the hybrid nature of the Prius, having read about its incredible fuel efficiency. He was also intrigued by how as big a man as Steve would cope with what was widely held to be a limited range on the telescoping adjustment on the steering wheel. Steve then added that he would have Carol with him anyhow and she would enjoy spending time with her old neighbour. This confused Alan, who thought he meant that they would have Joan in the car too, but once this was ironed out, the men agreed it was good plan and they would see each other at 1.00 on Wednesday. Alan was pleased about the arrangements on numerous counts, and after he had rung off, hummed lightly to himself as he continued his restock.

Yvonne was waiting for them on the steps, dressed strikingly in an emerald-green jumpsuit. She had tied her hair in a jaunty emerald headscarf, which set off her faux gold and jade earrings. They were clusters of spirals that tinkled gently as she moved her head and Carol commented on them straightaway.

"Oh, I love your earrings! Aren't they lovely?"

Yvonne beamed, touched one of the earrings in a pleased way and graciously thanked Carol. It set the tone for the afternoon. Normally Yvonne set up her bookings, made sure everyone had everything they needed and then left them to it, but today she hovered. Did they need an extension cable? Did they know where the toilets were? She and Carol struck up conversation whilst the men set up the tables and quickly discovered they had friends in common and by the time she had accepted and eaten a slice of Carol's Lemon Drizzle Cake, they had exchanged numbers with a view to Yvonne possibly joining Carol's book group. The group had recently dropped to only 5 and Carol was going to make enquiries to see if they might be ready for a new member, but she told Yvonne not to get her hopes up as it would be a group decision and some of them were a little set in their ways. Yvonne understood and said she didn't want to upset the applecart, but if there was space, she'd be thrilled, then realised what time it was and went back to work in her office.

Meanwhile, Senior Model Makers was a great success. They had four chaps from the home and a further three from outside. With Alan and Steve, that took them to 9, which was a very respectable number. They didn't count Carol as she didn't participate in the actual model making, but everybody agreed that the Lemon Drizzle was really good so she didn't feel left out. They had banked on possibly six so they were pleased at having to fetch another table and more chairs from the side room. The light was excellent in the hall and the models that Steve had chosen and Alan donated were perfectly suited to the occasion. Younger (under 70s) participants helped older participants where necessary and the older participants allowed themselves to be helped, which was a minor miracle. Alan put it down to the softening effect of Carol's fabulous cake, which melted away reserve and produced fuzzy feelings of wellbeing. Well, in him, anyhow.

Chapter 37

Yvonne returned just as everyone was packing away and could see, with her work hat on, that the meeting had been a success. She had not had to call an ambulance, nobody had come stumping along to her office to complain and the furniture was still intact. She could also see a contented glow around the men as they stood, delaying going back to their rooms or the growing evening dark of the outside world. Several models were still out, in progress, on the tables, and she leant in, the better to marvel at the detail and skill involved.

"These are going to be quite something," she said to the group at large. The men couldn't help but smile a little. They thought so too, and didn't need her to tell them, but it was nice all the same.

"It's a lovely hobby isn't it? I'm really glad we could get you fitted in for today. Is it a better day for you - it seems like there's more here this week?" She looked to Steve.

"Yes, absolutely. Thanks for changing it Yvonne. Best thing is, Alan here has been able to come. He's the chap that has The Model Shop? Donated the kits?"

"Oh yes, you said. Hello Alan."

Alan smiled and nodded in recognition, but quickly added, "Well, its not *my* shop, I'm just care taking it really. It belongs to my friend Martin. Martin Rundle. He's in New Zealand."

"Oh yes! Not long till he gets back now is it? I've been following him on Facebook. I love all his posts! That one with the white water rafting was dynamite!"

"I didn't realise you knew Martin, Yvonne?" said Steve.

"Oh, no, I don't, but a friend said I should look at his page," she tittered, "he's quite the pin up boy at Flower Club. Not many men his age look that good in a wetsuit!" She winked at Carol, who smiled bravely. Nobody else knew what to do with that information, but Yvonne was unfazed.

"Come on everybody, time to pack away, they start setting up for dinner at 4 o'clock. Chop, chop." Everybody was glad to oblige.

Steve, Alan and Carol were rounding up the last of the boxes and tools by the time Troy and Nathan arrived. They had been first to Joan's room, where they had found Ernest fast asleep on Joan's bed. Ernest always woke immediately when the boys came in, but Joan took a little more rousing. The first time they had been in this situation, the boys had slightly panicked and backed out into the corridor, assuming the worst had happened. Luckily, Kindly Tea Trolley Lady had intercepted them before they rushed off to the nurses' station to report a death. They were now completely used to Joan's shallow almost imperceptible breathing, delicate blue-tinged skin stretched tight around her open mouth and limp bird-like hands upon the covers. Ernest thumped his tail at them, but it wasn't until he took a daredevil leap off the bed and knocked a cup and saucer of cold half-drunk tea off the side table in the process that Joan proved she was still alive.

"Oh! Have you come for the cooker?" she asked querulously.

Nathan and Troy exchanged glances.

"Er, hello Joan. It's us, Nathan and Troy? We've come to take Ernest for his walk."

"Ernest? He's not here I'm afraid. He's at a funeral."

"Oh. I see." The boys looked at Ernest, hopping from foot to foot by the bedside and lapping up the tea. Nathan bent and picked up the little dog.

"Oh, he's back. Ready for your walk, Ernest?"

"He loves his walks, don't you Ernest? You are a good to take him." She started looking for her handbag.

"Pass my bag would you Martin, there's a good lad," she said, continuing to rifle through the bed clothes.

"Is this it, Joan?" asked Troy, holding the bag towards her.

"Oh yes, well done. Now, let me see, you must have something for your trouble." She went deep into the many folds of the interior.

"No, really Joan, it's fine, really," attempted Troy.

"Here we are!" she declared triumphantly, "now, one each, no fighting," she continued as she offered out a bag of icky old boiled sweets. At least they were wrapped this time.

The boys took one each, thanked Joan profusely and escaped with Ernest in tow.

*

"Boys! Just in time! Here, Nathan, carry this box would you?" asked Steve.

"Yeah, sure. Where's it going to?"

"That one's going to the Prius, Yvonne said there's a shed outside where we can leave some of the other things, but we need to get the key from her office. She's here until 4.30 so we should be okay," Steve replied.

"Is this the room you were thinking of, Grandad?" asked Nathan, as they paused to wait for Carol to put the remains of her Lemon Drizzle back in its Tupperware.

"Yes, yes. What do you think?"

"It's perfect isn't it? And like you said, those doors could go straight on to a marquee or tent or whatever. We could get loads of people in here. Maybe even 400?"

"Let's not get ahead of ourselves Nathan. 251 is all we need, but yes, I agree, there is certainly the potential for more."

"What does Yvonne say about it, Steve? Did she say yes?"

Alan and Steve exchanged glances.

"I haven't actually asked her yet," admitted Steve.

"Right well, come on then, let's go and ask her now." Troy was already walking towards her office as he spoke, with Ernest leading the way.

Before anybody could even come up with a plan, Troy had shot ahead and was knocking loudly on Yvonne's door.

Yvonne, professional as ever, was not even slightly put out by two teenagers, a dog and three older people piling into her office at 4.15 on a Wednesday. She accepted a second slice of Lemon Drizzle and listened carefully to their proposal. Troy said afterwards he was sure she would say yes as soon as he saw her post-it wall.

"She's one of us," he had said rather enigmatically.

She didn't say yes however. She asked a great deal of sensible questions, took copious notes and explained that it wasn't solely up to her. She would need to check with the owners, the insurers and the residents themselves to some extent. There was bound to be disruption to their routine but she could also see the benefits of hosting a community event on the premises. She did all of this in under 12 minutes, and at 4.29, she stood up, brushed the crumbs off her trouser suit and had them all out in the corridor as she locked the door behind her.

"I'll let you know by Friday lunchtime," she said, popping the keys into her rafia weave handbag and swinging it by its plastic gilded handles, she clopped off down the corridor.

Chapter 38

Thursday was Yvonne's day off, and normally she would stop by and visit her mother in the morning, reserving the afternoon for her own pursuits. She liked pottering in her immaculate garden in the summer months but was currently working on a macrame pot holder. She had been looking forward to really getting to grips with it and had additionally lined up the new Alfie Boe album, *As Time goes By* for her listening pleasure. She'd fallen for him heavily, back in 2007 when she'd gone with her sister Annette to the Music of Morse concert in the Albert Hall. She'd followed his career keenly ever since and going to see him in *Les Mis* and getting his autograph had been the high point of her adult life so far. She quite liked Michael Ball too, but not in the same way.

Yvonne had very clear boundaries when it came to work and home life, and made it a rule not to let either intrude on the other, but so invested was she in the proposed World Record Attempt that she had decided to make an exception. She phoned her mother and excused herself from visiting, made herself a coffee and logged in to her work account, confident she would be done by noon and ready for her appointment with Mr Boe and a ball of jute string at 1 pm.

On Friday morning, wearing a garnet-coloured jacket that she reserved for special occasions, she made her call to Steve. Steve alerted Alan, who used Facebook Messenger for the very first time ever to contact Martin, and Claire found out from Martin's Facebook page whilst scrolling through on her coffee break. By teatime, Troy and Nathan were all over it and already had 96 'definites' signed up. Steve set up a WhatsApp group called "World Record Breaking Attempt Participants" or WRAP for short and once Alan had been persuaded that it wasn't a scam or would cost him anything, he joined the group and arranged to host a real life meeting at the shop on Saturday morning, to include refreshments provided by Carol and a possible guest appearance by Yvonne, if she could duck out of Pilates without incurring a late cancellation charge. Claire would definitely be there, but had to leave by 11 in order to fit in the gym before collecting Matt from his Year 10 Battlefields trip, due to return to South Mimms Services at 1 o'clock. He could have stayed on and been picked up at school at 2 pm like everyone else, but he had to be at a hockey tournament in Hemel Hempstead by 2.30 and everyone agreed that would be cutting it too fine and Claire's fitness in preparation for her Police Bleep Test could not be compromised.

All of this information was shared, discussed and commented on painstakingly on the WhatsApp group. Alan was frankly exhausted by the attention it demanded and only Daisy's kindly intervention - showing him how to mute the group - made it possible for him to concentrate fully on the actual meeting when it finally began at 10 am on Saturday morning.

The meeting itself was only mildly less exhausting, as Troy had got Martin on Skype on his laptop, balanced carefully on the counter. There was much marvelling about the time difference (11 pm! He'd already had Saturday!) and the miracle of modern communication which meant that it was almost 10.30 am by the time they began anything of note.

Martin was keen to be there, obviously, and was due back on the 11th of December, which meant that before Christmas was a distinct possibility, but only just. Claire had been accepted onto the Detective Constable Degree Holder Entry Programme with Bedfordshire Police - a fact already known and celebrated within her immediate family - but as her starting date was February 12th she had to explain to the meeting at large why she would not be available after this date. A lot of people were surprised, in a good way, and a lot of people were not surprised, also in a good way, and nobody resented Claire taking a few moments to explain her life choices, but it did slow down the pace of the meeting. Claire spoke eloquently about the support she had received from her father, not just now, but throughout her life, and went on to specifically praise Nathan for encouraging her to follow her dream, an accolade that made him physically shrink but inwardly grow. He was beyond proud of his mother but had made her promise early on that she would never collect him from school in a squad car. She had gone, in a few short weeks, from wondering tentatively, about perhaps, maybe, becoming a PCSO to the realisation that her Chemistry degree and varied life experience could actually be the gateway to the career she had always dreamed of - an actual Detective Constable, specialising, she hoped, in Roads.

*

They all agreed it had to be a Saturday and this left the 22nd of December and the 26th of January as the only realistic possibilities, due to the many personal commitments of the assembled group. Troy and Nathan were keen to crack on and ride the wave of enthusiasm they had already generated and go with the 22nd, but the more mature members all urged caution, taking their time and generally not rushing anything, plus a generalised worry about it being 'too close to Christmas.' Frustration fizzed in Troy as he countered again and again for an early date, but he was overruled by the majority. Alan was just gathering everyone for a formal vote, well, less of a vote, more of a forgone conclusion, when the door pinged melodramatically. It was Yvonne, looking stunning in a sapphire-blue leather blouson jacket and slick leatherette leggings. Some of the men who didn't know her were clearly overwhelmed, either unable to look or indeed look away, sure she must be in the wrong shop.

Steve stepped forward, gallant as ever and guided her over to the Humbrol stand where Carol was waving cheerfully. Alan waited till everybody had settled down again then explained where they were with the date. Yvonne listened with interest. She closed her eyes, visualising the pastel post-its. Everyone waited, her close neighbours fascinated by the way her leaping dolphin earrings trembled in time with her heart beat.

"26th of January you said? It's a non-starter. Can't be done. We've got the new radiators being fitted, it's been on the cards since March last year. Contractors start on the 23rd of January, it's a massive job. It won't be finished for at least three weeks, let alone in 3 days, by the time they've had the floors up, re-routed the pipework and replastered. 22nd of December, however, no problem at all."

Alan inhaled deeply and looked around at the heady mix of experience, enthusiasm and very specific skills in the room.

"All those in favour of the 22nd of December?"

Nathan and Troy punched the air immediately, disturbing the static air around them.

There were glances, hands in pockets, hands scratching chins and hands firmly folded under forearms as everyone thought about it, but like a seismic wave, the enthusiasm of the two boys worked its magic as first one, then another hand joined them, until there was no doubt that the World Record Attempt was very definitely happening on the 22nd of December, just two weeks away.

Chapter 39

People left the meeting feeling as if there was a huge amount to do, but could not put their finger on what there actually *was* to do. Yvonne had arranged all the permissions and insurance and so on for Foxholes and Troy and Nathan were already up to 132 participants by the close of the meeting and felt confident that they could easily get the numbers up to the required to 251 through social media alone. Alan had volunteered to speak to his contact at *The Comet* and cover those people locally who still bought a weekly newspaper. He silently planned to email the television news team at *Look East* as well, but he didn't want to get anyone's hopes up too much so said nothing.

The air began to still and settle as everybody steadily filed out, leaving Alan alone with his clipboard and the dog. They looked at each other briefly before Ernest sighed and turned his attention to washing his undercarriage, which he had been prevented from doing during the meeting.

Steve was taking care of the World Record Attempt paperwork. As he had explained to the group, he'd done the initial research and submitted the application already, so now that there was a date, he could really get going. The key to having the record verified was evidence and Steve had spoken seriously about how they would need to ensure that their evidence was sufficient and correct. He proposed sending out the roles required on the WhatsApp group, and it wasn't that long before Alan's phone was alive with comments and responses to the information supplied. They would need two witnesses who were not associated with or related to the record organisers, as well as an independent timekeeper and marshalls to make sure the correct protocols were observed on the day. Everyone Alan knew was going to be associated with or related to the record attempt, so he could not imagine who would take on these crucial jobs, but luckily, no model maker is an island.

By teatime, they had signed up the coach from Hockey Club to be the timekeeper, one librarian and a court recorder to be witnesses and at least eight marshalls had volunteered, including two from the Police call centre and three Tesco employees from the one near where Steve lived, not the one in town.

Martin set up a specific Facebook group, tentatively called "Big Model Event", but he was advised early on to change the name as there was concern that this might be misconstrued, and he settled on "Guinness World Record Attempt for the most people building aircraft models at once Group." Not catchy, but clear.

It had also been left to Martin to source the models. They all agreed that it ought to be possible to get a company to donate the kits for free, working on the basis that they would get a huge amount of publicity and kudos, especially if they were able to break the world record. Martin had contacts spread far and wide throughout the industry and was frankly glad of something else to do in New Zealand. He had definitely 'caught up' with Gerry now and they were almost at the awkward chin tilt/tight smile stage now. Having picked up his hire car in Auckland, he had gone up to the beaches of Northland and back down by plane to Wellington, then flown out again to Marlborough for a wineries tour before whale watching, bungee jumping and zip wiring his way back to Christchurch. He had planned to spend the last week or so following the West Coast Wilderness Trail by e-bike, and kayaking up the Punakaiki River, but as long as he could get Wi-Fi in the evenings, there was no reason for him not to take on this important role.

*

Martin had certainly come a long way since he had left the UK. The flight had been pretty much as expected, with thankfully not even a hint of the awful dream he'd had the night before his departure. There had been a slightly tense moment at Dubai, where it looked as if he might be sitting next to a large sweaty lady with teenage twins, but thankfully they had been upgraded and he was left with an empty seat next to him for the longest part of his journey. It had given him time to reflect, not only on what exactly he was going to fill his time with in the coming weeks, but also longer term. The shop was very much on his mind, but he realised that if he was to get his full money's worth from New Zealand, he would have to mentally step away from his responsibilities at home, just as he and Alan had agreed. Martin had spent so long blocking out uncomfortable or unwelcome thoughts over the course of his life, that this would be second nature to him, and he immersed himself fully into all the country had to offer.

Gerry had been tremendously welcoming and very much as he remembered him, and spending time with someone who had known him as a boy, as a young man, had made him realise that he was not just this old man that he had become. Gerry cracked open the wine, they sat on the deck, ate prawns off the barbecue and life was good. On his second evening there, Gerry had been reminiscing about the numerous camping trips they had taken, both with Scouts and as an intrepid duo. Martin found it hard to reconcile his current largely indoor and very risk-averse lifestyle to this pre-teen persona that had been happy to hunker down in the pouring rain, sheltered only by a wispy tent made from an old washing line and his mother's second best spare room bed sheet. He remembered very clearly being allowed to camp overnight in the garden with Gerry from about the age of six, maybe seven, including making their own breakfast (beans initially, then later bacon, eggs and sausages) on what must've been - he, Gerry and Mr Google now realised - one of the very first Campingaz stoves available in the UK. They had both loved Scouts and had competed to 'out badge' each other, revelling in the range and depth of experience that working towards a new badge offered. Martin, never one to willingly throw away what might otherwise be catalogued and stored, was deeply impressed when Gerry trotted inside and returned not only with his camp blanket complete with 67 badges, but also his Bob-a-Job card from the year he turned 12. Gerry showed Martin the completed card, with all the usual helpful tasks such as lawn mowing, wood chopping and car washing recorded in various types and colours of ink, but the grand finale, for which he earned 2 'bob' (about 10 pence now, they marvelled) was 'Chopping Concrete.' He and Martin had both been involved in this particular job, but Martin had mentally buried it in a brain pile marked 'Shameful incidents' and flushed now at the memory. One of the lads from the troop, Don Huntley they recalled, had a neighbour called Mrs Sands, who had asked for help. She had taken against her patio as an unwelcome reminder of her husband who had recently run off with the girl from the newsagents'. Mrs Sands had bravely tried to remove it herself with a small hammer, but it had taken the combined forces of pretty much the whole Scout troop to obliterate it and lob the offending concrete over the fence and, unknowingly at the time, it must be said, onto the railway sidings below. At twelve, they hadn't given much thought to what might have been over the other side of the fence, but they both agreed that Don Huntley would have known, but he never said a word; that was him all over.

There had of course been repercussions and the following year there had been better supervision. But still, happy days!

Remembering times such as these roused something long forgotten in Martin. He had after all been a concrete lobber and it was with the spirit of a youthful adventurer that he had set off on his travels around New Zealand. Exhilarated by healthy exercise, majestic scenery and memories of causing major havoc to all trains in and out of his home town for at least 24 hours, he was able to dash off an average of 17 emails each evening, and was very quickly able to report back to the group that he had secured 300 kits, for free, from a leading manufacturer who was proposing to dispatch them within 3 to 5 working days, in plenty of time for the 22nd December. He'd negotiated hard and was ultimately happy with the 1/72 Spitfire MK Vb they had offered. He explained to the group at large that although he would personally have preferred the MK11a, the Vb spinner would, he conceded, add interest for the more experienced modellers whilst causing no significant difficulties for the amateurs and first timers the event would no doubt attract. The group agreed.

Chapter 40

Martin applied the handbrake firmly and turned off the radio. He'd had the heating on full (funny how quickly he had become unaccustomed to lower temperatures) and so reached out to replace the grey plastic slider back into its customary central position. He turned the key decisively to stop the engine but let it rest in the ignition and returned his hands to the wheel. The car quieted around him, the engine making gentle ticks as it settled. The key fob gently swinging was the only movement and Martin focused on the small to and fro it made until it stopped. He was home. He was exhausted.

He eased himself out of the car and walked around to the boot to gather his case and trundled it over to the front door. The doormat was starting to curl at the edge and he poked it with his toe, not sure if it had always been like that or had happened in his absence.

The house smelled a little musty and felt still and unused, but once he was satisfied that there had been no leaks or incursions, he made himself a herbal tea, took his case upstairs and slept the sleep of the travel weary.

It was nearly 10 by the time he got to the shop the following day. Alan had been expecting him since opening but he'd been rushed off his feet and hadn't really noticed the time, so when the door opened and it was Martin, he felt immediately flustered. He knew he was apprehensive about Martin's return, despite Claire's reassurances and Martin's own obvious enthusiasm by Skype at the meeting on Saturday, but even he was surprised by how much Martin's presence threw him. Over the last five weeks, the shop had become a home from home for him. It wasn't his, he knew that, and yet...

"Martin!"

"Alan!" Martin kept one hand on the door handle, and the other holding his laptop bag.

"Come in! I mean, you don't need me to tell you to come in. Good to see you!"

Martin was looking around the shop now, noticing the changes big and small. Ernest wagged his tail repeatedly but didn't get out of his basket.

"So, the posters, the battening is easily removable as you can see from the clips I have attached to the cornicing. They can be easily removed, it hasn't marked the paintwork at all, as you can see," Alan twittered, as he followed Martin's gaze up and around the walls.

"I've kept everything where it was. Well, we had to move everything when we had the launch day, oh, yes, I see you've met Avalar..." He paused while Martin looked the mighty cardboard cut-out almost in the neck, his natural line of sight being several inches below the glowing red eyes, "but we took photos and I think it's all back to where it was."

Martin remained silent, carrying on a mental inventory and physical tour. Finally he spoke, "I notice you're running out of Light Buff there," he said, pointing to the Humbrol stand.

Alan cursed inwardly. The one colour he'd not been able to restock fully.

"Yes, absolutely, the suppliers were supposed to send it last week, but it got missed off the order. Should be here tomorrow, fingers crossed."

Martin raised an eyebrow.

The phone rang, slicing through the silence. Alan looked at the phone, Martin looked at the phone. Alan wanted to answer the phone, Martin wanted to answer the phone. Martin fixed Alan in the eye for the briefest of beats, Alan couldn't take it, stepped sideways and in one smooth movement Martin was back on the plinth, laptop bag neatly at his feet.

"Hello, The Model Shop. Martin Rundle speaking."

A strained silence ensued. It felt like forever but it was no longer than it took for Alan to inhale nervously and look away.

"No, it's Martin Rundle here, the proprietor, may I help you?"

A second physically painful silence for Alan.

"I see. Yes, of course. He's right here." He turned towards Alan, "it's for you."

Things warmed up over the remainder of the morning and luckily both men were pros at being polite and carrying on as if nothing was wrong and by lunchtime they were both sufficiently convinced that everything was fine. Martin closed up the shop with Alan itching in the doorway, wanting to *not* say anything, but also very aware that he had discovered that if you shut the toilet window *after* turning off the kettle plug socket instead of *before*, you could save yourself retracing your steps.

It was a pleasant walk in the crisp blue-sky winter sunshine to the pub where they had booked to have lunch and effect the official handover. Ernest alternately strained on his lead to get ahead and stopped dead the better to gather interesting smells he could pee on. The men waited patiently whilst he avoided their gaze. It was the pub where Martin had always gone with Joan and the staff were pleased to see him and Ernest after so long and also wanted to know all about where Joan was. Martin related the full story, Ernest was made much of and there was a general agreement that Foxholes was a nice place and the staff all asked Martin to give her their regards when he explained that he would see her after lunch. They planned to get there in time not only to see Joan, but hopefully introduce Martin to Yvonne and catch up with Steve at Senior Model Makers Club. Lunch was pleasant and reasonably priced and although it wasn't prawns on a barbecue, Martin appreciated being there with Alan, and grudgingly, perhaps Ernest too.

Alan still felt bad about the vast amount of money the shop had made in Martin's absence, but if Martin was upset or offended about the massive increase, he certainly gave no sign of it. He accepted what had happened and they briefly discussed the negative implications for tax purposes before moving onto the World Record Attempt, a topic which engaged and interested them both immensely. Numbers were good, the kits were coming on Friday and the article in *The Comet* was both prominent and factual, although Martin was surprised to see Carol in the photograph. Alan explained how helpful she had been and her offer to coordinate the refreshments, plus her connection to Steve who was doing the World Record Attempt paperwork. Martin looked at him just a moment longer than necessary - was there something else he wasn't saying? Alan blushed.

"Nice lady, Carol," offered Martin.

"Yes, yes, she is," Alan replied.

Chapter 41

I t was all very jolly when they got to Foxholes. The home had been decorated for some weeks, but they had just got the Christmas tree up in the foyer and some of the residents were helping to decorate it. Yvonne was with them, wearing a suitably festive ruby-red jumper and black flared trousers with smart red boots. She waved as Martin, Alan and Ernest came through the doors and then clopped over to see them, her fingers still laden with baubles and a rope of tinsel flicked elegantly over her shoulders.

"Hello all, hello in person, Martin. We have met on Skype but I must say, it's not the same," she paused fractionally and looked him up and down. On Facebook, he had seemed small in comparison to the majestic mountains in the background, but in fact, here in the foyer, without the mountains, he was still small. Which was fine. She went on, unflustered as ever, "and welcome to Foxholes. I'm Yvonne."

"Thank you, yes, good to meet you too. I understand you will be masterminding, or should I say, mistressminding, the arrangements here?"

Alan took an involuntary step away from Martin. If ever anyone could make a perfectly ordinary situation awkward, it was Martin. Yvonne, however, was unfazed.

"Absolutely. It's all going to plan so far. Housekeeping staff are on board and the vast majority of our independently mobile residents will be out on the Christmas lunch trip to the garden centre, leaving us free rein in the hall until 4, which, I'm sure you'll agree, should be ample time to achieve a World Record." She smiled brightly and checked her co-ordinating Swatch watch. "If you'll excuse me gentlemen, Ernest, I must get on." She turned to the group around the tree, who in her absence had started to drift away in every direction from the glare of the tree lights, like shy woodland beetles.

"Come on everybody, let's get this tree done. And you, Mrs Bede, we need your critical eye. You'll tell us if it's not symmetrical won't you?' She fixed Mrs Bede with a challenging look and leant over to grab her wheelchair handles, spinning her round to face the tree again.

Yvonne had an interesting relationship with Mrs Bede. When she had first arrived at Foxholes some years ago, Yvonne's heart had lurched at the sight of her name on the registration papers. Mrs Patricia Bede, could it be the same Mrs Bede that had taught her English at school? 'Patricia' gave no clue. Yvonne was of a generation that could not possibly have imagined a teacher with a first name, but surely, *that* Mrs Bede would be long gone by now? She had been ancient when she had taught Yvonne, or at least ageless. A person in tweed with a firm grip on the class, an encyclopaedic knowledge of English Literature and a clear disdain for makeup and personal grooming.

On her arrival, Yvonne had reverted to her fifteen-year-old self and hidden in her office, biting the edges of her fingers. She'd flagged down the manager as she passed the door, asking for details of the new occupant of room 15. The manager confirmed that this Mrs Bede must indeed be the same Mrs Bede. Yvonne would have to face up to this blast from the past in the way she had learnt to face up to everything - she would have to take control. She popped open her compact mirror, reapplied an expert heavy slick of lipstick, checked her pineapple earrings were front facing and tugged her citrine-coloured scarf into a more confident angle, then picking up the weekly events schedule flyer, she set off for room 15.

Mrs Bede never stood a chance. She was caught unawares, concentrating deeply on rearranging her extensive handkerchief collection in the too-small chest of drawers that came as standard issue. Mrs Bede's poor hearing and Yvonne's silent arrival (she'd slipped her trainers on before leaving the office, thinking ahead as always) gave Yvonne the added advantage of being able to eyeball this powerhouse of a woman who had been such an awe-inspiring part of her school days before she turned round and noticed her.

Yvonne noted her attention to detail, her focus on the task in hand and saw that although the wheelchair might signal frailty to a casual observer, Mrs Bede was exactly as she remembered. She would play it cool.

"Knock, knock," trilled Yvonne as she knocked. "Mrs Bede? Hello, my name is Yvonne, I'm the entertainments lead here at Foxholes, and I thought you might like to look over the schedule for the week?"

Mrs Bede looked up, a little flustered for a moment, then, her brain catching up with her senses, she pinned Yvonne in her sharp blue gaze, but didn't reply.

"Mrs Bede? My name is Yvonne, and as I said..."

"I know exactly who you are dear. Yvonne Humbert, shocking handwriting but showed promise in creative writing. Used to sit next to that Emma girl, the one that was captain of everything, what was her name?" She looked down to gather her memories.

"Emma Standish? She works in London now, PR for a sports equipment firm."

"Ha, yes, Standish. Her older sister was a terrible show off, but Emma was a worker. Sister was called Helen, I believe, wanted to go to RADA or some such. Suits a show off, acting. Obviously came to nothing, I've never seen her name in lights."

Yvonne paused, thinking of everyone's best interests.

"No, she never did become an actress."

She could have added "because she committed suicide, having struggled with mental illness throughout her teens" but this wasn't the moment. Mrs Bede didn't know everything.

Chapter 42

Joan was delighted to see Martin again, but primarily because she had just dropped her handbag on the floor and was having trouble recapturing its myriad contents.

"Oh Martin, be a dear would you? It's my silly old hip, I just can't get about like before. Terry's been wonderful, visits every day, but of course he can't be here all the time, he's got to keep the business going you know."

Martin mentally logged that she had not registered his five-week absence, that Terry had been dead for almost 2 years or that the business had folded in 1978. He wisely decided not to challenge anything and instead led with a hearty "Hello Joan!" and let Ernest divert her attention.

"Oh stop him, Terry, he's got a tissue! Don't let him have it, it's a filthy habit, Ernest, you are a naughty boy, stop it at once!" she twittered from her chair. Ernest took no notice but Martin gingerly took what remaining tissue he could out of the little dog's mouth, and then lifted him up onto Joan's lap. She was so thin now that Ernest struggled to find purchase with his paws and it was a few moments before he had hoovered up some stray crumbs from the front of her cardigan and was able to settle. Martin was shocked at the deterioration that he saw. Yes, she was thinner but a part of her had drifted away. She still looked like Joan, but her edges lacked clarity and her focus was off. She had had her hair set by the in-house hairdresser and although Martin could not have said what was different, it didn't look like Joan's hair. The hairdresser was lovely and had such a nice way with her, but she really only had two hairstyles to offer and she had chosen 'Old Lady Curls 2' for Joan, who had previously had her beautiful white hair swept back into two combs away from her face. Her hair was clean, it was tidy, it was obviously cared for, but it wasn't Joan.

They chatted about this and that for a while and Kindly Tea Trolley Lady came clanking past in the corridor outside. Ernest hurled himself off Joan's lap, following the promise of biscuits with his special walk, leaving Martin and Joan alone. Joan gave Martin a long history of one the carers that he hadn't met and it was just like old times, except that suddenly, it wasn't.

"Martin, tell me, have I upset Sheila?"

Martin sat very still, thinking what to say.

"No, no, I don't think so Joan."

"Only, she hasn't been to see me. Have I upset her?"

"No, you haven't upset her." He avoided her gaze and looked out through the window and beyond her to the great trees in the parkland.

"Well, is she poorly? She didn't look very well when I saw her last. Is she not well Martin, is that why she hasn't been? She's ill, isn't she Martin. What's the matter? What is it?"

"She's, well, yes, she, don't you remember, Joan? What happened?"

Joan stilled, time stopped, her face crumpled and slow tears spilled from her blue eyes. She raised her fragile hands to her face and spread her thin fingers over her cheeks. Her mouth gaped, caught in freeze frame by misery and despair.

Martin looked down at his shoes, watching his own tears refract on the shiny leather of his toecaps.

"Martin. Martin. My girl, my beautiful girl, she's gone." The words escaped her, leaving her spent and spare.

"Yes Joan. Sheila's gone. She went a long time ago now."

He reached out and took his mother-in-law's hands from her face.

She gripped his hands tightly, her sobs becoming quieter and more internal, as she drew back into a place that was less solid than reality and far more distant.

"I'm so tired, Martin, so very, very tired."

"I know."

Martin sat with her until she drifted into a gentle sleep. It was starting to get dark outside, making the trees into magnificent silhouettes, and the kind evening light seemed to take the years away from Joan, so that Martin was reminded of the vivacious, kind, resilient woman she had been. Just like Sheila.

They sat, companionably and yet worlds away, until the nice tea trolley lady flicked on the light and clanked the trolley in.

"Oh, look at you two, sitting in the dark. Nice cup of tea, Joan? And one for this handsome young man. Is this your boyfriend Joan?

"Oh, you are a card! This is my son-in-law, Martin. Martin this is.... she looks after me, don't you? Martin's just got back from, where was it Martin?"

"Oh, you're that Martin! I loved those pictures of whales you put on Facebook. You must have been ever so close. Weren't you frightened? I would have been terrified!?"

"Well, no, I actually wasn't that close. I do have a telephoto lens on my digital camera, but it was tricky getting them off my SD card and into the format I needed for Facebook, so actually, I found that my phone produced surprisingly good results."

Kindly Tea Trolley Lady had zoned out by this time, and luckily Ernest reappeared to save her having to come up with a response that feigned interest.

"Here he comes, little beggar. Well may you wag your tail, young man. Caught me off guard he did, got the whole lot of Mrs Steele's bourbons *and* the pink wafers I was saving for room 11."

They all looked at Ernest fondly.

"Well, I can't stand around here all day, I've got to get on. See you later Joan, nice to meet you Martin. You coming with me then, trouble?"

Ernest and Kindly Tea Trolley Lady left the room. Martin stood and brushed down his trousers.

"Right, well, better get on, Joan."

"Yes, yes, off you go. Give my love to Sheila."

Martin paused. "Yes, I will."

Chapter 43

There had been some discussion on the WhatsApp group that an in-person meeting might be necessary on Friday evening, the day before the World Record Attempt, but everybody could see that all angles were covered and it would be more beneficial to meet early in the morning before the event started to discuss the day's schedule. Three hundred kits had arrived as promised and Martin was in charge of getting them to Foxholes, which he had done after closing on Thursday. Steve had dotted every i and crossed every t regarding the official world record attempt and they were all confident that as long as they got the numbers on the day, the record would be theirs. Nathan and Troy had come up trumps and had 274 confirmed entries, and Claire had thoroughly enjoyed liaising with the Foxholes caretaker and creating a foolproof parking and one-way system. Tony, of Sing with Tony, was going to do the PA system and additional tables and chairs had already been delivered by the Scouts, ready to be erected by them on Saturday morning. Carol had made twelve Lemon Drizzle cakes by Thursday lunchtime and liaised with Yvonne who had made a lovely laminated pricelist (with clipart) for the teas and coffees.

They were not charging for the event, as per the rules, but had agreed that donation buckets would be visible and all monies raised should go to Models for Heroes, a charity brought to their attention by Ken, one of the Senior Model Makers Club, himself an ex-serviceman. Ken's son Alastair had struggled on leaving the forces and he'd been signposted to M4H, who had not only provided him with kits but allowed him to meet with others in a similar situation who also found model making to be a curative hobby. Nobody wanted to talk about 'mental health' but they all knew that model making was important for them and could imagine how it might help others.

Nathan and Troy had felt that 5.30 was too early to meet, but they had been overruled by the collective voices of wisdom around them, and so, bleary eyed and slightly stunned, the team gathered at Foxholes, arriving in cars or on foot (or carried in Ernest's case, it being too cold and early for walking) and crunching over the frozen gravel to congregate by the rear entrance as instructed. Their breath gathered and clouded under the security lighting, the gentle burr of coughing, shuffling and muttering the predominant sound. At exactly 5.30 the light came on inside and the sound of multiple locks being opened attracted their attention. Yvonne swung open the door with her immaculately manicured hand (Rich Amethyst nail polish to compliment her purple joggers and hoodie) and invited them to begin the day.

Residents were being treated to breakfast in bed and so the hall was free. The Scouts were not due until 8.30 to put up the tables and the large empty space before them filled the assembled company with a degree of awe and wonder. People started to mill uncertainly, not sure where to start. Alan waited for Martin to step forward and call everything to order, but Martin didn't. Martin was deliberately faffing with the banner he had had printed, some gaffer tape and a tape measure. Yvonne was talking animatedly to Carol, clearly not about anything of importance, he felt, as he could see Carol laughingly hysterically and then looking at Steve, who was standing at some distance, quietly, with both his hands in his pockets.

Two sharp whistle blasts brought everyone's attention to Claire, who had brought her own milk crate and was standing on it purposefully.

"Thank you ladies and gentlemen. And welcome! It's wonderful to see you all here and thank you for all the hard work you have already done. Today is a big day, as you know, and I just wanted to run through the plan. Nathan and Troy are handing out clipboards now - thank you to the PE staff at school! - with the schedule on the front and a complimentary branded commemorative ballpoint pen, kindly donated by one of our sponsors, APC Print, thank you Michael!" A tall bearded man gave a comedy curtsey and a couple of ragged cheers came from those nearby.

"Please take a moment to familiarise yourself with the running order. Any questions so far?" She didn't imagine there would be, everything was clear. There were no questions.

"Right, housekeeping," Claire went on to cover all the important relevant health and safety points and enjoyed watching the whole room swivel to note the emergency exits, here, and here, as she pointed her hi-vis clad arm.

"As you will see, we have designated 6.15 for the first coffee and tea of the day, thank you Carol and team," (another ragged cheer) "and if you could use the time until then to collect your appropriate tabards and bring in anything you may need from your vehicle now to avoid later congestion." She paused as Yvonne came over and touched her arm then whispered something into her ear.

"Could the owner of registration Kilo Uniform 61 Victor Foxtrot Foxtrot, a silver Toyota Prius, please move their vehicle as it is blocking one of the emergency exits? Thank you."

Steve flushed to the roots of his remaining hair and, grabbing his coat, left as quickly and discreetly as possible, to yet another ragged cheer.

*

By 9.55, absolutely everything was ready. The banner had gone up beautifully, much to Martin's relief, and Andy reported that the car parking system appeared to be faultless, much to Claire's relief. The doors were due to open at 10 sharp, with participants being registered at the door, then shown to a numbered place at one of many tables set around the hall. Whilst lots of those already inside the hall were planning to participate they had been given clear instructions to leave the hall and re-enter and register, just like everybody else, and so there had been a coordinated exodus at 9.45 to allow them to go and gather in a specially roped-off area (thank you Claire) which allowed them priority access, but not until 10 o'clock. It had been explained to those already queueing that this would be happening and people were largely understanding of the situation. Model making would not begin until 11 o'clock, giving everyone a chance to settle, use the facilities and possibly have tea and cake.

*

Nathan and Troy had been dashing up and down the queue with their tally click counters, Ernest in tow, and whilst their enthusiasm and jumpiness meant that they could not agree a specific total, it was definitely over 200 already. 251 was the magic number, but it was still early.

At exactly 9.58, Claire took her milk crate and megaphone outside.

"Good morning model makers!" she announced dramatically, clearly expecting a big response.

People shuffled and greeted her politely, but she wasn't happy.

"I can't hear you! I said, good morning model makers!" Nathan died just a little.

The crowd gave a grudging but more acceptable "Good morning."

"That's more like it! Are we ready to make some models?" she bellowed.

Some braver souls shouted "Yes!", but the general response was underwhelming. Claire pressed on.

"You can do better than that! I said, are we ready to make some models?" Nathan went to go back inside, prepared to lose his place in the priority area.

Luckily, Alan moved forward and tapped his watch meaningfully at Claire, clearly carried away by the megaphone. She'd have to keep her eye on this sort of thing once she was a Police Officer, but he supposed they taught them 'that sort of thing' at training.

The doors opened behind her, and the priority access group filed neatly in.

"Please allow those in the priority access area to enter the building first, thank you ladies and gentlemen. Thank you, please enter the building, thank you. Let's break a record!"

The event had begun.

Chapter 44

I t might have been supposed that the 274 expected participants would be pretty homogeneous. Men of a certain age, a smattering of youths and perhaps one or two ladies wearing very sensible footwear, but this was very much not the case. The first through the door, apart from the priority access group, were in fairness, older and stereotypical and excited little surprise in Martin and Alan who were registering at a table by the door. Martin seem to know most of them by sight or reputation but Alan had to keep himself from going down a rabbit hole of partial recognition every time somebody gave him their details. Lots of people he didn't know greeted him by name but once he realised this was probably because he had a name badge on, he relaxed a little. He nearly lost his nerve when he found himself registering the lady from the Day of the Mince, the one who strongly suspected him of being a paedophile, but he stayed calm and although she hurried her young son into the hall she didn't actually say anything or even look at him that suspiciously. Hopefully, she had moved on.

He took a break about 40 minutes in, and stood back to watch the flow of people filling up the numbered spaces. There were grandchildren, children and young people of all ages, milling around the adults they had come with. The youngest looked to be about six or seven, which concerned Alan. They'd put a minimum age of eight on the event, largely due to the glue they were using being unsuitable for the under 8s, but also because they weren't sure that younger children would be able to complete the models independently, and that was vital for numbers to count towards the record. Alan discreetly asked Claire to make enquiries. He didn't want to be seen to be asking young children how old they were. She reported back that the child in question was indeed eight, a fact that the parents had been able to verify by showing photographs of said child in Cubs uniform, something he would not have been confident to ask for.

At the other end of the scale, there was a good turnout of residents from Foxholes, including Len Hatton, the home's oldest resident at one hundred and two. Len was sprightly and had only just stopped jogging on a daily basis, but he was accompanied by his son, a portly man in his late eighties who clearly needed to sit down at regular intervals and Len was bustling round trying to find him a chair.

Hayleigh, the receptionist from the dentist, had rather weirdly sent her apologies and dropped a five pound note in an envelope into the shop with the message "To Mr Barnwell, hope the record attempt goes well, Hayleigh." explaining to Martin as she handed it over that she'd seen it on the Internet. It was unclear what she thought was going on.

Allison was there with Daisy and her two little friends who looked like they were having a whale of a time. There was much hilarity and hooting coming from their table, which included Alan's newsagent and his niece who was a regular at the shop since the launch. Had he been able to name them individually, he would've noted Tyler, Sam, Charlie, Jahaan and Saul from Troy and Nathan's school Model Club, but he simply saw 'youths' joshing and generally being a bit silly but in a nice non-threatening way, with Ernest lashed securely to their table and gathering up any crumbs or otherwise that they might drop. He was unerringly able to identify the person most likely to feed him in any group situation and had centred his efforts on Jaahan, who was slipping him Quavers on a regular basis. The table next to them included several girls who had also been at the launch, as well as several girls who hadn't. Some of them affected boredom and stared at their phones, but careful observation by Claire, who recognised 'Chloe-two-visits' from launch day, showed them to be very aware of their surroundings and the effect they were having on the neighbouring table. Things escalated briefly when an empty crisp packet was thrown, but Claire swooped in and picked it up, putting a stop to further interaction between the tables.

A group from the sixth form college was there, a whole table of Tesco employees and another of paramedics, both in their respective uniforms, and a number of teachers from school including Mr Peterson, he of the dual personality and Model Club Leader. He was accompanied by a seriously glamorously dressed unnatural blonde wearing an immaculate white trouser suit, high heeled tan and white co-respondent shoes and a wide-brimmed white hat, last seen being worn by Kid Creole circa 1982. Could this be Loony Susie, wondered Alan? She didn't look particularly unhinged, just an extremely tall person who was clearly out of Mr Peterson's league. However, as Nathan remarked, she also clearly wasn't entirely sane if she was with Mr Peterson.

By 10.50, numbers were at a very satisfying 284, comfortably over the 251 necessary to beat the Hendon record. Some people had dropped out, to be sure, but others who had not preregistered had turned up on spec and been welcomed in. Claire was just doing a final announcement in the car park when she stopped in her tracks.

"Carl. What are you doing here?"

"Hi, Claire. Yeah, so, I hope it's okay for me to be here?" He scratched his stubble.

"It's a public event. Anyone can be here. But why would you want to be here?"

"Yeah, so, Matt messaged me, I'm meeting him here?"

"Matt messaged you?"

"Yeah, we've been, you know, messaging. He's just been a bit held up at…"

"Yes, at hockey practice. I know." Claire cut him off, gaining the upper hand once more. "Doesn't finish till 11 o'clock. This event starts at 11. If that's why you are here.'

"Yeah, so, they said he could leave a bit early? He'll, oh, he's, hi Matt, mate, over here!" called Carl.

Matt waved in acknowledgment and stowed his bike messily by the wheelie bins, covering his embarrassment at surprising his mother with this overt meeting by fiddling with his bike lock. He juggled his bike helmet and hockey stick, rucksack and water bottle for a few seconds before Claire called out, "Put it in the car, Matt," dangling the keys for him to fetch. He dropped everything and jogged over.

"Thanks Mum," he looked sideways at his Dad, "Hi Dad."

"Matt! Mate! Good to see you!"

They both watched him gathering his possessions and manoeuvring them into the boot of Claire's car.

"Can't believe you've still got the Audi, Claire."

"Yes, well, if you look after things, they last." She paused. "As I said, it starts at 11. You've still got a few minutes before they close entries. Does Nathan know you're coming?"

"Yeah, he's kept us a place I think."

"Alright then Dad? See you inside Mum."

Claire watched them go and then, taking a deep breath, she followed them inside, closing the doors firmly behind herself.

Steve had marshalled the room, given the last words of encouragement and instruction, and as the clock ticked over to exactly 11 o'clock, 286 people began to build their models.

Chapter 45

The rules required each model to be completed, but did not specify to what standard. The general consensus was that it had to have used all the parts in the box and have the relevant decals applied. No painting was required for these specific kits which one or two participants were disappointed by, and they raised this with the Marshalls, who went to fetch Claire. Claire handled it all very smoothly, in such a way that the complainants went away feeling like superior but benevolent beings, prepared to accept the limitations of the lesser mortals around them, rather than a couple of pernickety nuisances who had failed to read the small print on the entry form. She was good like that, having had years of practice.

On completion of their model, participants had been asked to turn their entry card over to display the reverse side, still numbered but with a bright green background. Alan and Michael, the printer, had agonised over this detail, torn between red, signifying the end, stop, I have completed the task and the more positive green for Go! One more to add towards our goal of completion. As they looked around now at the growing sea of green cards, they both felt that they had made the right choice.

There was a brief kerfuffle just after 11.00, when it was discovered that Ernest had broken free of his shackles and was at large in the room. Several people had their bags searched by him and although nobody actually complained, there was some awkwardness from one gentleman about the loss of a packet of Starbursts. Alan was called over to adjudicate and was able to de-escalate the situation by starting an animated discussion about when and why Opal Fruits became Starbursts.

Just after 12.00, the Marshalls began exchanging significant looks and at 12.16, Steve was called over. He listened to their huddled reports, nodded several times and went to ask Claire for the megaphone and milk crate. People began to nudge each other and a ripple of tension went through the refreshment queue, people uncertain if they should return to their seats or stay where they were. Some people who were sitting stood up, and some who were standing sat down, but by the time Steve was atop the milk crate he had everyone's attention.

"Ladies and Gentlemen, boys and girls, I have just received some news from our Marshalls." He looked down at his clipboard, as those nearest to him peered over to see what he was reading.

"I have to tell you that at 12.16 today, the 22nd of December 2018, we reached a total of 251 completed aircraft, thus exceeding the current world record."

Cheering, applause, some whooping and a little light stamping greeted this announcement.

"However, however, it is our aim for all 286 of you to complete your models. This will ensure that our record stands for as long as possible. Please allow for those who have yet to finish to do so, but let us allow ourselves a small moment of congratulation. Three cheers for the new World Record Holders!"

Within the hour, Steve was reaching for the megaphone again. Everyone knew what was coming. Nothing but green cards, every table, every number, each in front of a completed model aircraft. Some of them were a bit wonky to be sure, but some of them were superb. For the record, they were all the same. Each one represented something amazing to its owner. Maybe it was their first model, made hesitantly next to dad or auntie, maybe it would be their last model treasured as such by those they would leave behind. Maybe it was the first time they had made a model alongside someone else, maybe it was the last time they would ever leave the peace and solitude of their own shed again and put the whole thing down to an unpleasant experience. Yes, everybody there had made a model, but they had also all made a memory, good or bad. Some people had also made connections, made tentative eye contact and even made exchanges of phone numbers, in the happy case of Nathan and Chloe-two-visits. Everybody had spoken to somebody, sat next to somebody and been part of something big and important feeling.

"Ladies and gentlemen, I am delighted to inform you that today, 286 of you have completed a model aircraft kit simultaneously." (Huge cheer) "I have asked our Marshalls and Timekeeper to record and verify this, and it only remains for us to add in the all-important photographic evidence. Could you all please return to your seats and await direction from our photographer?"

The photographs took some time as there was an issue with the lighting. Happily, Tony, from Sing with Tony, was finally able to put his glitter ball to good use and everyone praised his ingenuity whilst Martin readjusted his tripod. Martin held the room to stiff attention and took the necessary pictures to prove that 286 people had indeed each made a model aircraft at one time and at one location.

Documentation was everything.

"Thank you, ladies and gentlemen." Claire took back the megaphone. "Just a few thank yous before we all head off." She went through a long list of people, each of whom hated being singled out but would have been deeply upset not to be mentioned. People started to reach for their coats, stowed under tables and chairs, and gather their bags and models. The Scouts piled in and expertly dismantled, lugged and removed the tables and chairs. Within 15 minutes the hall was empty except for the people (and animal) that had made it all possible.

Coats on, no chairs remaining, they stood in a sort of circle, blinking and inhaling, each clutching their own model.

"So, we did it!" said Yvonne to the group, jangling her purple bangles as she jazz handed at everyone generally.

Martin raised a steadying hand.

"Now, let's not get ahead of ourselves. We did have 286 models completed, and I know that the paperwork and evidence will prove that," he smiled at Steve, "but it's not a done deal until it's verified, as you know. Twelve weeks is the time scale they give. It's not an (he did the air quote thing with his fingers) 'official' world record until we get the certificate."

Nathan and Troy exchanged glances. Alan noticed and smiled.

"Of course Martin, but I think we might allow ourselves a modest celebration, don't you think? Quick cup of tea before they come in to set up for the evening meal everyone?"

Yvonne and Carol exchanged glances.

"I think we can do better than that, don't you Carol?" beamed Yvonne, nodding at Carol.

"Now?" said Carol.

"Yes, Carol, now," agreed Yvonne.

Carol scuttled off to the kitchen area and returned carrying a massive cake of her own making in the shape of a Spitfire. Yvonne tinkled after her and brought back a tray with glasses and two bottles of chilled Cava.

"Martin, would you do the honours please?" she said, handing him the first bottle.

"Of course," he replied, taking the neck of the bottle. Their fingers brushed for the briefest of milliseconds, but it was enough for Martin to be forced to acknowledge that today had truly been a success on every level.

Chapter 46

The March wind blew hard down the High Street and as Alan and Ernest came through the door of the model shop, it followed them in, gusting and tugging at Alan's coat, and rustling the papers that Martin was poring over on the counter.

The framed certificate stood proudly in prime position on the wall directly behind the plinth. It gave Alan a thrill to see it every time he came into the shop and it was fresh enough to be a constant talking point with every customer.

"Good morning, Martin! It's a windy one, for sure!" he began, as he wrestled off his coat and went to put it on the pegs. Bending down, he unclipped Ernest's lead. Ernest went straight to his basket in the window, turned around several times and flopped dramatically down.

"Indeed it is," replied Martin, rearranging the papers and putting them in a sturdy brown envelope with Alan's name on it.

"They said on the weather about high-sided vehicles having to take care," ventured Alan.

"Indeed. I believe that warning only applied to certain areas far North of here. I don't anticipate any issues with my motorhome, if that's what you are implying."

"Of course," said Alan, somewhat chastened. "So, she's looking good out there Martin. I like what you've done with the rear bike carrier. Really sturdy looking. Tell me, will you be able to charge your e-bike on the RV?"

"It's not an RV Martin. It's a motorhome. But, yes, I will be able to charge my e-bike from the motorhome, as long as I do not leave it unattended whilst doing so."

Alan recognised Martin as being in a highly anxious state and attempted to placate him.

"So, the modified bike carrier, was it a big job?"

"Well, yes and no. Obviously the e-bike needed a slightly heavier gauge set-up than the one supplied as factory standard, and although it was a considerable effort to make the modifications, once I worked out how to do it, it was fairly straightforward and I think it was worth while."

"Hmm, you might even be able to get two e-bikes on it, d'you think?" ventured Alan, knowing that he was pushing Martin's buttons and that Yvonne had also recently got an e-bike.

Martin didn't rise to the bait.

"It's clearly designed for two bikes Alan, did you not see the second rack, directly behind the front one? The motorhome itself has ample room for more than one person and it would have been shortsighted of the manufacturers not to allow for two bikes, E or otherwise. And in fact, the manufacturers refer to it as their 'Couples' model." He paused, feeling as though he'd said something indelicate. "Although as a solo traveller, I shall enjoy the extra space that implies."

"Of course." Alan, slightly giddy with it all, felt like sniggering but thought better of it.

"So, are we all straight with everything then, if you're setting off now?"

"Yes Alan, we are. The beauty of the motorhome is that I can choose my own itinerary, go where my interests take me and be at one with nature."

They both looked at Ernest in the window, gently snoring.

"Of course, yes. But if you booked the site for a 2 o'clock arrival, hadn't you better go, soonish, or you'll get caught on the M25 surely?"

Martin looked over the top of his glasses.

"I may well get caught on the M25 Alan, but I can leave at any exit I choose, find a safe place to park up and wait it out in the comfort of my own vehicle," announced Martin grandly.

Alan stood on the pavement in front of the shop door watching as Martin reversed the motorhome out from the designated parking space and drew to a halt alongside him. Ernest strained on his lead, keen to get to the bollard. Martin settled himself in the driver's seat, lowered the sun visor against the weak spring sunshine and checked his satnav one last time. He lowered the motorhome window and turned towards Alan and Ernest.

"Alright? Not changed your mind?" smiled Alan nervously.

Martin smiled. "I just wanted to say, I'm really pleased it's all worked out, you know?"

"Me too. Good Luck and Bon Voyage Martin!"

He watched him merge into the morning traffic, indicate left at the lights and disappear. He was drawn back into the present by Ernest's insistent whistling. He sighed contentedly, looking at the little dog at his feet.

"Yes, alright, give me a minute," he said.

Alan re-erected the bollard, waited for Ernest to pee, and then, jangling his shop keys jauntily, they stepped purposefully into the model shop, ready to begin.

About the Author

Christine has spent her career working with children and animals. After qualifying as a primary school teacher and SEN specialist, she moved into Alternative Provision, where her days ranged from taking a corn snake named *Kellogs* to Nottingham in a pillowcase, to lying on the floor designing assault courses for mice. These experiences taught her, first-hand, the extraordinary power animals have to connect with people.

Her extensive experience with neurodiversity has shaped her deep belief that our differences should be embraced and that life is richer when we truly accept one another. Writing has always been her way of making sense of the world, but this is her first full-length story.

Christine lives in Lincolnshire with her husband, her two dogs, Otto and Roy, her cat Purdy, and a revolving population of rescue chickens.

Acknowledgements

I would like to thank the following people, without whom this book would never have been completed:

My daughter, Jen, whose constant encouragement to keep writing, and eagerness to hear each new chapter read aloud, has been a powerful motivating force.

My son, Fred, whose unwavering belief in my ability as a writer has inspired me to carry on.

My writer's circle, who have shown me that my work is worthy of an audience, with special thanks to Jo Parfitt.

My proofreader, Susan Boyd, who brought fresh eyes and invaluable clarity to the manuscript.

All my beta readers: Sarah Kirby, Christina Utilini, Emma Cose, Louise Bradley at Stamford Library and Tamara Hartley, as well as those who offered encouragement with their positive feedback, in particular Sue Blunt, Mary Hoyle and Rachel Larder.

My mother, Jenny, who always believed in me and taught me to love reading.

And last, but by no means least, the real-life Ernest the late and great: "Bertrude, Lord Bertrude, 3rd Earl of Bertrude", the dog of my heart, and the best dachshund ever.

www.ingramcontent.com/pod-product-compliance
Ingram Content Group UK Ltd.
Pitfield, Milton Keynes, MK11 3LW, UK
UKHW021312151025
8408UKWH00013B/86